"It is hardly necessary to reminisce about all the foolish things we once said to each other."

"I agree. We both had a tendency to talk too much. We still do."

And, leaning forward, he silenced her with a swift kiss. As he gathered her in his arms, she felt the familiar thrill course through her that Jared's kisses had always been able to induce.

Hot, passionate, seeking, his embrace was as she'd remembered and yet ... There was a tenderness to Jared's kiss that had never existed before, that not only stirred her blood, but branded itself into her heart as well.

THE
VALENTINE'S
DAY BALL

Susan Carroll

FAWCETT CREST • NEW YORK

A Fawcett Crest Book
Published by Ballantine Books
Copyright © 1994 by Susan Coppula

All rights reserved under International and Pan-American Copyright Conventions. Published in the United States of America by Ballantine Books, a division of Random House, Inc., New York, and simultaneously in Canada by Random House of Canada Limited, Toronto.

Library of Congress Catalog Card Number: 93-90715

ISBN 0-449-22210-1

Manufactured in the United States of America

First Edition: February 1994

Chapter 1

Awakening to the sight of a grinning Cupid would be enough to give any man apoplexy. And not one, but a half dozen fat cherubs, danced in front of Sir Jared Branden's bleary-eyed gaze, their deadly bows and arrows all pointed right at his heart.

With a low groan, Jared rolled over, burying his dark head deeper into the pillow, closing his eyes, trying to dive back into the blessed realms of unconsciousness. It was of no use. He became more fully awake by the minute, more aware of the throbbing in his head, a sour taste in his mouth, all unpleasantly familiar sensations, the consequences of a night of too much merriment.

After several moments, he emerged from the pillow with another soft moan and forced his eyes open. Mercifully he discovered there weren't really six Cupids inhabiting the bedchamber with him. As he managed to focus, they blended into one. But that was bad enough, he thought, shuddering at the sight of the painting of the plump winged god with rosy cheeks.

"Who'd hang a monstrosity like that on the wall?" he muttered. And then another question more pertinent penetrated his sleep-fogged brain. "Where the devil am I?"

He didn't expect an answer, but he got one.

"At Silversby Manor, Warwickshire, monsieur." The voice, long-suffering and icy with disapproval, echoed from somewhere near the foot of the bed.

Jared shifted painfully, squinting at the trim form of his valet. As wretched as he felt, Jared couldn't suppress a small feeling of triumph. His valet, Frontenac, was a sanctimonious prig, the more unbearable because the fellow was near perfect and almost always right.

But Monsieur Frontenac was definitely wrong this time, because as hung over as he was, Jared was damned sure he wasn't in Warwickshire. He was in London. Hazy memories flitted through his head of gaming at White's, blotting his name in the betting book, slipping on the ice-covered sidewalk at the corner of St. James. And then . . .

Other memories crowded forward. A coach. Horses. Leather reins gripped in his hands. Oh, God! Another soft groan escaped Jared. Could Frontenac possibly be right again?

Silversby Manor, Warwickshire?

Jared's eyes roved over the chintz trappings of the unfamiliar bedchamber. There was only one way to settle the matter. He shifted the coverlet and sheets away, no great feat since the bedclothes were already slipping off the hard-muscled contours of his naked form.

He noted Frontenac turn to face the other direction. By some quirk, Jared thought wryly, he had managed to acquire the only Frenchman in the history of Gaul who was a prude. It still outraged his valet that Jared chose to sleep in the nude, but it was a habit he had acquired after a pistol ball had lodged itself in his thigh, cutting short his military career. During his long convalescence, Jared hadn't been able to abide the feel of any nightshirt tangling about his legs. He still couldn't.

Though that wound had long ago healed, his right leg continued to betray him, as it did now when he attempted to lever himself off the bed. The room spun crazily as he hugged the bedpost for support. For a few horrible seconds, he feared he was going to cast up his accounts. But he had a constitution of iron that had seen him through worse things than a night of excess.

Taking deep breaths, Jared willed the nausea to pass and the carpet to steady beneath his feet. Pursing his lips, Frontenac held out Jared's wine-colored dressing gown. Jared took it from him and shrugged into the garment, belting it about his waist.

He caught a glimpse of a gilt-trimmed ornate mirror hanging opposite. The sight reflected back to him was not a pretty one. Eyes that should have been a rich mahogany seemed to be swimming in a sea of red. Strands of ebony hair straggled across the brow of a lean face, pale beneath a stubble of beard, a face that this morning was looking too haggard for a man of thirty-two years.

Covering his eyes, Jared gestured mutely towards the mirror. As one long practiced in obeying such silent commands, Frontenac padded forward and covered up the offending object with a towel.

Only then did Jared limp over to twitch the primrose curtains aside. Sunlight stabbed at his eyes and he cursed. Gradually he was able to take in the full scope of the scene outside his snow-frosted window.

A bucolic garden complete with hedgerows gradually sloped away to become a rolling country landscape powdered with white.

"Damn. It *is* Warwickshire," he mumbled, letting the curtain fall. Turning away from the window was almost as painful to his throbbing temples as facing Frontenac's smug expression.

Jared sagged onto an armchair. "How in the devil's name did we get here?"

"You drove us. In the carriage, monsieur."

"I drove? What happened to Benton?"

"The coachman wisely elected to remain behind in London, monsieur."

Jared started to grin, then winced, even that small effort causing his head to pound. "Benton always was a coward. You quite surpass him for valor, Frontenac."

"Only because I couldn't get the coach door open in time to flee, monsieur."

Jared leaned his head back against the chair, sighing and rubbing his forehead. "It was a wager, I suppose? I seem to recollect that much."

"Yes, monsieur. You undertook to drive a coach and four to Warwickshire in less than three hours."

"Did I make it?"

"Oh, yes, monsieur." Frontenac gave an expressive shudder.

"That's a mercy at least," Jared mumbled. He supposed he had done stupider things when in his cups than race a carriage hell-bent for leather over night-darkened, icy roads. But he couldn't recollect any at the moment.

One thing, however, continued to mystify him.

"Why Warwickshire?" he mused aloud. "Why would someone even dead drunk want to race to Warwickshire?"

"Your uncle lives here. The Earl of Brixted."

"I know that, fool. That's all the more reason I wouldn't want to—" Jared broke off, an unwelcome thought occurring to him. "Oh, Lord, I didn't come to borrow money from Uncle Charles, did I? I won a tidy sum at White's the other night. Never tell me I lost it already."

"No, monsieur. I kept a close guard upon the winnings."

"Good man," Jared murmured with relief. Trust Frontenac to keep the purse strings pulled tighter than the lacings on a spinster's corset.

The news heartened Jared enough that he was able to face the prospect of the day ahead, the confrontation with his uncle that awaited him. He didn't need any of Frontenac's colorful descriptions to figure out the state he must have been in when he arrived at Silversby Manor last night. Nor did it take any great stretch of the imagination to predict his uncle's reaction. The earl had been quite an old rip in his day. But Jared had discovered that no one could deliver more self-righteous lectures on proper conduct than a reformed rake.

He longed for nothing more than to collapse back into bed, pull the pillow over his aching head. But he supposed the hour must already be well advanced, and a late appearance would only make his reception from his uncle that much more unpleasant.

As though to prepare his master for this grim interview, Frontenac laid out Jared's most subdued tailcoat—navy blue, severely tailored, modest dark buttons. Considering his abrupt departure from London, Jared would not have been astonished to discover that he did not have so much as a change of cravat with him.

But Frontenac, with his usual air of irritating superiority, appeared to have risen to the occasion. Somehow he had not only managed to pack upon such short notice, but he had done so with his usual precision, not a single crease appearing in Jared's white linen shirt or buff-colored breeches.

Moving with the silent grace and efficiency of a cat, the valet soon had Jared shaved and dressed in his shirt, waistcoat, and breeches. By the time Jared tugged on his own Hessians, the thunder in his head had subsided to a dull ache. He felt presentable enough to risk removing the towel from the mirror.

Better, he thought, eyeing his reflection with a grimace, but not much. Even with his dark hair smoothed back from his brow and his angular jaw clean-shaven, he still didn't quite present the appearance of a gentleman. Maybe it was those raffish lines time had carved about his mouth. Or maybe it was the jaded cynicism that years of hard living had filtered into his eyes. He looked like a man paving his way to hell so fast, he was likely to beat the devil home.

Jared experienced a brief flicker of shame, self-contempt, but he had long ago learned to overmaster both emotions. Only in the folly of his youth had he given himself over to considerations of what grand things he meant to do with his life. These days he concentrated on more important matters, like the style of his cravat.

As he arranged the white stock about his neck, he was pleased to note that his hands were steady. During this delicate operation, Frontenac stood back respectfully, holding Jared's coat in readiness.

The silence of the great house surrounding him almost unnerved Jared. He was accustomed to the bustle in London, the constant barrage of noise from the streets outside his lodgings in St. James. He'd always found the country deadly dull by comparison, and once again he wondered what had possessed him to come haring into Warwickshire.

As he carefully made the first crease in his cravat, he growled, "It's so infernal quiet here, you can hear the damned clocks tick. Is it Sunday?"

"No, monsieur. Thursday. St. Valentine's Day."

Jarod's fingers froze for a moment, then he softly cursed his valet for reminding him. "I'd actually managed to forget the date."

"Indeed?" Frontenac sniffed. "I was certain monsieur was well aware of what day it is."

Jared angled away from the mirror enough to scowl at his valet. "And just what is that supposed to mean?"

"Only that I have observed that it is monsieur's habit every year on the eve of St. Valentine's to become a little too . . . er, convivial."

"The devil I do! I don't do anything by habit."

"I do not wish to seem impertinent by correcting monsieur," Frontenac persisted, "but every St. Valentine's Eve since the six years I have had the pleasure to be in monsieur's employ, monsieur has always consumed a too large portion of brandy."

"What do you do? Keep a log of my jug-bitten sprees?"

"Of a certainty not, monsieur. But your pattern in this has been so marked, one could not fail to notice."

Jared glared at him before turning back to the mirror, his irritation with Frontenac nearly causing him to ruin the lines of his cravat. Jared foxed every St. Valentine's Eve? His valet was quite mad. Even if it was true, then it happened by pure coincidence and not by any design on Jared's part.

To admit that he purposefully became drunk every February thirteenth would be like admitting he had some upcoming dread of Valentine's, as though the day were associated in his mind with some haunting memory. Oh, he had memories, all right, but he refused to concede that they caused him any pain.

Carefully making another fold in the cravat, he muttered, "I'd wager there are many men who drink themselves insensible at the thought of St. Valentine's. It's a ridiculous holiday."

"It is the day for *amour*, for romance, monsieur. Surely you, who take such interest in the ladies—"

"My interest in ladies has nothing to do with romance or love," Jared said bluntly. "I've never had any patience for all this hearts-and-flowers nonsense."

"Then it is unfortunate that monsieur chose this occasion to visit your uncle."

"Why is that?"

"Because I have gleaned from the servants belowstairs, there is to be a ball held at the manor tonight, in honor of St. Valentine."

Jared let out a heartfelt groan.

"Also to announce the betrothal of his lordship's youngest daughter."

"Impossible. Uncle Charles surely must have all those dratted girls married off by now. I suppose it must be what's-her-name, the little fubsy-faced one."

"Your cousin Caroline, monsieur."

That was another annoying thing about Frontenac. With little effort, he seemed able to recall all the names and conditions of Jared's sundry relatives, a feat Jared had never been able to master. But then he had never given himself the bother.

Finished with tying the cravat, Jared paused to study the flawless result he had achieved. He reached up and deliberately rumpled some of the folds. No sense giving the mistaken impression that there could be anything perfect about Sir Jared Branden. Besides, there was always the amusement of hearing Frontenac's pained sigh.

As the valet helped Jared ease the tight-fitting coat over Jared's waistcoat, he instructed Frontonac, "Don't bother with any more unpacking. I'm damned if I'm hanging about for any St. Valentine's ball."

"Very good, monsieur," Frontenac said dourly.

"We'll be gone as soon as I pay my respects to my uncle. They keep country hours here, so I suppose I am too late for any breakfast."

"Oh, no, monsieur. It is barely ten of the clock."

9

"What!" Jared paused to stare at the man. "That's practically the crack of dawn. Why didn't you tell me it was so early?"

"It was not my place to say," Frontenac replied, smoothing the coat's fabric over Jared's broad shoulders. "Monsieur seemed so eager to rise."

Something perilously near a smirk marred the valet's impassive features. Jared swore silently. He was going to throttle the man with his bare hands someday. He'd likely be tried and hanged for murder, but it would be worth it.

Shrugging away from Frontenac's ministrations, Jared headed for the door, determined to get the upcoming ordeal with his uncle over with.

As he crossed the threshold, stepping into the hallway beyond, his right leg gave a painful twinge. The surgeon never had been able to remove every shard of the exploding mortar shell that had nearly cost Jared his leg. A fragment remained imbedded deep in his bone, a macabre sort of souvenir, a curious kind of barometer.

His leg had a tendency to throb at any hint of a change in the weather or impending storm. But it was no storm that awaited Jared in the hallway. It was a vision.

He paused, sharply drawing in his breath. A woman carrying a lace paper heart had just emerged from her own bedchamber two doors down. Sun streaming through the oriel window at the end of the hall backlit her golden crown of hair, giving it the effect of a halo, the simple lines of her high-waisted white gown becoming like the robes of an angel.

She turned slightly, starting at the sight of

Jared, and he gazed at delicate features, achingly familiar. Maria Addams was no longer a schoolgirl, but her face possessed a timeless beauty, a sweet old-fashioned loveliness that put Jared in mind of legends of flaxen-haired maidens that lured silvery unicorns from dark secret forests, inspired knights to take arms against fire-breathing dragons, gave voice to the songs of troubadours.

He blinked, astonished to discover that he had that much poetry left in his soul to conjure up such images, astonished even more that Maria Addams could still have such an effect on him.

Not Miss Maria Addams, he corrected himself wryly. The Contessa di Montifiori Vincerone.

Their eyes locked for a moment in silence, hers the hue of those first fresh violets of springtime. Her lips trembled, and for one mad second, he almost believed she meant to smile at him. But no, that would have been entirely too much to ask for.

Maria drew herself up stiffly, whipping the valentine she carried behind her back. "Branden! What—what are you doing here?"

Maria's grace seemed to make him all the more conscious of his ungainly limp. But he managed to sweep her a credible enough bow.

"What am I doing, Lady Monty—" He never had been able to get used to calling her by that preposterous title. He concluded smoothly, "I am merely standing here, struck dumb by your beauty, Contessa."

"That would be a novelty," she said tartly. "You know what I mean. What are you doing *here* at Silversby? You never visit your uncle. If I had imagined for one moment that you would do so, I I would have—would have—"

"Taken care to be a thousand miles away?"

"No, a mere hundred would suffice, and I should think you would feel quite the same, sir."

"That is where you have always wronged me, my dear," he drawled. "I have never sought to avoid your charming company. Actually, it seems singularly appropriate that the fates should have thrown us together on today of all days."

"And why is that, sir?" she asked with a brittle smile.

He pressed one hand to his heart, striking a wounded posture that would have done credit to Richard Kean. "Can it be you have forgotten? St. Valentine's Day. The tenth anniversary of the day you jilted me, left me waiting in the pouring rain at the church door?"

"Oh, hush, you fool!" Maria cast an anxious glance down the hallway. "Do you want the whole household to hear you?"

"It's an old scandal, my dear, and not a very remarkable one. Come to think of it, it wasn't even much remarked upon when it was a new scandal." He fetched a deep sigh. "There was no one present to witness my humiliation except the good Reverend Belcher and his wife."

"It was all your own fault. I told you—" she began hotly, then checked herself. Shaking her head, she gave a rueful laugh. "No, you shan't do this to me again, sir. We meet but rarely, yet every time you provoke me into a quarrel, raking over old coals. Well, at least one of us now has too much dignity for that."

"Yes, but don't fret over it, Contessa," he said kindly. "I'm sure you'll also acquire some in time."

Those fine blue eyes looked daggers at him, and he supposed it was ungallant of him to bait her this way whenever they chanced to meet. But when she adopted that regal manner, calling him "sir" in that cool, distant fashion, it never failed to rouse the devil in him.

He couldn't help noticing how furtive she was being about that valentine she carried, keeping it whisked behind her back. In a spirit of pure mischief, he attempted to peer around her.

"What's that you're hiding in your skirts?" he demanded.

"N-Nothing. I'm not hiding anything. Now, if you will excuse me, sir." She attempted to slip past him.

But Jared feinted left, then right, blocking her path.

"Stand out of my way, sir," she grated.

"Not until you show me what you have there."

"It's only a valentine! Now, are you quite satisfied?" She flashed the elaborately painted paper heart in front of his eyes.

"A valentine. But how charming," he purred.

Looking self-conscious, she was already attempting to hide the thing, but he caught her wrist, preventing her.

"There's an old custom that says the first man you see on St. Valentine's Day is supposed to be your sweetheart. Can this card possibly be for me?"

"Most decidedly not!" she said, attempting to squirm free.

"My dear Maria! You've seen another man al-

13

ready this morning? And you just emerged from your bedchamber."

"No, of course—that is, you know I haven't!"

"Ah, then you do intend the valentine for me. What a handsome gesture on your part. Finally letting bygones be bygones." He plucked the valentine playfully from her fingers, ignoring her indignant gasp.

"You will return that to me at once, sir," she commanded with an imperious stamp of her foot.

But Jared had never been good at obeying commands. That had been partly what had made his military career such a disaster. Besides, his curiosity was roused. It was rare these days to see the regal Maria blushing and looking so adorably flustered.

Could it possibly be she'd finally given over mourning for that foolish Italian count she had married? Had she decided to take a lover or another husband? She'd obviously expended a great deal of effort constructing this lace heart for someone, and all his teasing aside, Jared was damn sure it wasn't for him.

He limped closer to the oriel window, holding the paper heart up to the light. Maria rustled after him, but with her lack of inches, it was an easy matter to keep the valentine away from her. Holding it out of her reach, Jared proceeded to examine it through his quizzing glass.

"Damn you, Jared," she said, abandoning any further attempt at icy dignity. "Give that back to me!"

"How sentimental you are, dearest. It is quite

like old times with you calling me Jared and damning me again."

She expelled her breath in a furious hiss and made a desperate lunge for the heart, a maneuver he adroitly avoided. Though he had little taste for valentines, this one was exquisite. Maria always had possessed a large measure of artistic talent. She had decorated the heart with delicate floral sprays, a true lovers' knot entwined over the center.

He twisted it this way and that, but try as he might, he could discover no name to whom the valentine was addressed. Then he realized she had cleverly inked words through the loops and turns of the lovers' knot.

By this time Maria had given over trying to snatch the card back. She stood with arms folded, simmering. "You are no gentleman, sir."

"It took you ten years to discover that?"

"No, happily I figured that out before I was foolish enough to wed you."

"Touché," he murmured. By squinting, he was able to decipher some of the words entwined through the knot. He clucked his tongue. "Maria, the artwork is magnificent, but this poetry! You must have copied it out of one of those dreadful books like *The Complete British Valentine Writer*."

"I did no such thing," she denied, but she winced as he read aloud,

"You are my starlight and my dear.
I am like putty when you are near.
There comes but once a hero bold and true . . ."

He lowered his quizzing glass with a sigh. "Dear me. I get the feeling this wasn't intended for me after all. I am crushed."

"You will be very soon," she muttered. She extended one hand, trembling with suppressed rage. "Now, if you are quite finished, sir."

But still he held the valentine back. "If this isn't mine, perhaps I shall hold it for ransom."

"Sir Jared, please!"

"But if you were to ask me sweetly . . ."

"I just said *please*."

"Why did it sound more like 'Off with his head'? No, I fear I have something even sweeter in mind."

"Like what?"

"A kiss perhaps. If I'm not to have a valentine, I think I should at least receive some token. After all, it is our tenth anniversary of not being married."

He tossed out the suggestion with no other thought than to outrage her, and it produced the desired effect. Her gloved hands balled into fists, her eyes flashed blue fire, the color flew high in her cheeks. She looked magnificent.

But then her lashes swept down, veiling her eyes, and she forced her hands to relax. "Very well, sir."

"Very well what?"

"You shall have your kiss. Anything to put an end to this nonsense."

Her sudden acquiescence took him aback. But she was already gliding closer. He became conscious of the lace tucker trimming her gown, like a tantalizing veil whispering across the creamy swell of her breasts. The familiar scent of her lilac perfume filled his nostrils, making him a little dizzy. She always had been the most delightfully feminine woman he'd ever known.

As she rested her hands lightly on his chest, he felt an unexpected quickening of his blood.

"Now, I do have your word? If I kiss you, you will return the valentine?"

"Of course," he murmured. "You must remember that much about me. I may be a thorough scoundrel, but I never cheat at cards or on bargains I make."

She ducked her head, looking enchantingly bashful. "You've got to close your eyes. I can't do it if you stare at me so."

Intoxicated by the rise and fall of her breasts, the heady sweet scent of her, Jared closed his eyes and leaned forward, his mouth tingling with anticipation.

The next instant he received a hard blow to the cheek that made his eyes water. As he staggered back, Maria wrenched the valentine from him, half tearing it in the process.

"There," she cried in triumph, whisking away from him. "Unlike you, sir, I don't play fair anymore. I have learned to cheat."

In a flurry of skirts, she stormed back to her room and hurled herself inside, slamming the door behind her. Jared slowly straightened. Holding one hand to his stinging cheek, he gingerly tested his jaw. Damn, he wouldn't have been surprised to discover she'd dislocated it. He couldn't remember Maria being able to hit that hard. In fact, he couldn't remember her ever hitting at all. What had that

Italian husband of hers done? Given her prizefighting lessons?

It would seem that Jared's gentle maiden no longer waited for her knight in shining armor. She slew her own dragons these days.

"Ah well," he said. "In any event, happy anniversary, my dear."

Despite his sore cheek, his lips quirked into an unrepentant grin as he walked off down the hall. He kept the smile fixed in place on the off chance she might be peeking out her door.

It was only when he was certain he was out of view that he permitted the amused smile to fade. He couldn't help wondering what simpering fellow she'd made that valentine for. But more than that, he wondered why he should still give a damn.

Chapter 2

Slamming her bedchamber door closed, Maria leaned up against it for support. She clutched the precious valentine in her hands and was annoyed to discover her fingers were trembling from the rage of emotions Jared Branden had set loose inside her.

Damn the man anyway, Maria thought, blinking back furious tears. She had spent so much time and effort fashioning herself into the elegant Contessa di Montifiori Vincerone, a woman of cool and collected sophistication. But one teasing word, one maddening look from Jared, could transform her back into Maria Addams again, a flustered, stammering little schoolgirl.

After what had passed between them so many years ago, one would think the man would keep his distance, not make a habit of popping up when she least expected him like some wicked genie. Though in all fairness, Jared had looked equally stunned to see her this morning.

But he could have nodded politely and gone on his way, not stayed to tease her about their "anniversary." As if she needed any reminding about what had happened on that long-ago Valentine's

Day. Only Jared could be trusted to refer to such a painful episode in flippant terms. He always had possessed a knack for reducing even the most tender moments to the level of a jest.

But it didn't matter, she told herself fiercely. Jared no longer had the power to wound or distress her. He had taken her by surprise, that was all. Another time she would dismiss him with the icy disdain he deserved. She was no longer little Miss Addams wearing her heart on her sleeve.

She had discovered that the best hearts were those made of paper. They could be easily mended. Glancing down at her valentine, she was annoyed to see that it had been crumpled and torn during the struggle with Jared, some of the words smudged.

She was surveying the damage when her maid entered from the little dressing room that adjoined the bedchamber. Her arms full of Maria's frocks that needed mending, Alice Brewster drew up short at the sight of her mistress. Her broad, country woman's face peered from beneath the lace frills of her cap, her mouth puckered with concern.

"Milady! You are back so soon. And so pale! Are you quite all right? You look as though you have just fled from a hundred demons."

"Not a hundred, Alice, only one," Maria said dryly. "Branden is here."

"Oh dear. Shall I fetch the Hungary Water?"

"No, he didn't succeed in giving me a headache this time. Quite the contrary." Maria's lips curved into a tiny smile. "I gave him a sharp box to the ears."

"Oh, milady!" Alice murmured, looking profoundly shocked. The sandy-haired maid thought that a proper lady should always approach any gentleman with soft manners and modest, downcast eyes.

Just like Mama, Maria thought bitterly. Even when vexed, her mama had never done anything but weep prettily. Maria had fast observed that weeping prettily had never gotten her mother anything except more cause for tears. No, a swift box to a man's ears accomplished a deal more.

Alice set down the mending, still looking troubled by what Maria had told her. "Did Sir Jared offer you some insult, milady? Perhaps you should complain to his uncle, the earl. I am sure his lordship would not permit—"

"That is quite unnecessary, Alice. I have already dealt with Sir Jared myself. And he didn't insult me. He merely tried to steal my valentine."

"To—to steal your—" Alice's eyes went round. "Why would he do a thing like that?"

"I have no idea. He is not the least sentimental. He never had any interest in valentines even when we were—" Maria broke off uncomfortably. Some women made a practice of confiding everything in their maids, but Maria wasn't one of them. She had engaged Alice when she had returned from living abroad three years ago. Alice was not privy to Maria's broken engagement or any of the other secrets of her past, and Maria preferred to keep it that way.

She concluded by saying airily, "Whoever knows why Sir Jared decides to do anything? The man is quite mad."

"Mad?" Alice gasped.

Maria sometimes forgot her maid had a habit of taking everything that was said to her literally. A spirit of mischief stirred inside her.

"Yes," she sighed. "Sir Jared suffers from these bouts of insanity. His family occasionally has to keep him locked up, but most of the time, he is harmless enough. When he is seized with one of his mad fits, the only way to bring him back to his senses is a good hard box on the ears."

"Dear me!"

"You can always tell when a fit is coming over him. He gets a devilish look in his eyes and his mouth widens with an insane grin."

"I shall remember that, milady, and be sure to stay clear of him," Alice said. She shook her head and clucked her tongue. "I'd heard that Sir Jared could be a bit wild, but mad! I had no idea."

Maria felt a slight twinge of guilt for making up such tales about Jared. But if the man would persist in tormenting her this way, he deserved it. She did not know what mischance had brought him to Silversby Manor, but she refused to allow his presence to distress her any further. She had more important matters to think about. Such as her valentine.

Maria stalked across the bedchamber towards the dressing table. Although she'd only been a guest in the Earl of Brixted's country manor since yesterday, Maria had already managed to turn the little mahogany table into a clutter of jars of scent, ivory-handled combs, laces, fans, and dozens of gloves. Adding to the feminine chaos were her watercolors, paintbrushes, inkpot, and scissors.

Stripping off her gloves, Maria seated herself at the dressing table and prepared to mend the damage to the valentine. Alice rustled after her. The woman had hovered nervously at Maria's shoulder when Maria had made the valentine last night. Now Alice stood watching again, twisting her fingers in her apron.

Maria endured this as long as she could before saying, "Alice! Please stop wringing your hands. You make me feel as though I was constructing a bomb that could explode at any moment."

"I am sorry, milady. 'Tis only that I was thinking it might have been a mercy if Sir Jared had run off with that thing."

"It's not a thing. It's a valentine. And Branden stealing it would have been a disaster. He's the one person who might have been clever enough to figure out my secret code."

Not that it would have mattered if Jared had deciphered the code, Maria reflected. Even if he had become privy to her plans, with all his cynical indifference, Maria doubted that Jared would have attempted to interfere one way or the other.

But Jared had obviously thought the valentine's sentiments were genuine and intended for another gentleman. Though Maria could not have said why, it gave her a great deal of satisfaction that Jared should continue in his mistaken belief.

Alice drew in a deep breath and said in a pleading rush, "Oh, please, milady, reconsider. Don't deliver that there valentine."

"We discussed all of this last night, Alice. My mind is quite made up."

"I'm sorry, milady," Alice said miserably. "But I

am not accustomed to all this intrigue, secret codes and suchlike. The last lady I served was a very quiet woman, practically an invalid."

The late Lady Butress had also been a skinflint, leaving Alice nothing for all her years of devoted service but a cheap mourning ring. But Maria forbore to remind her maid of that.

As for the secret code Alice complained of, Maria regarded it with satisfaction. It was one of her cleverest efforts, she thought as she re-inked the words that had become smudged. The foolish poetry that Jared had so mocked concealed a message that was not so foolish, a message of hope, the promise of rescue and escape—

"Alice!" Maria exclaimed. Her nervous maid crowded so close, she had nudged Maria's arm, nearly causing her to blot the words all over again. Maria directed her a look of long-suffering reproach until Alice retreated to the fireside and took up some mending.

Maria bit back a rueful smile. Alice was a dear creature and very efficient. She supposed it was too much to ask that one's maid also possess a spirit of adventure.

Alice licked her thread and slipped it through the needle. Unfortunately, the activity did nothing to still her tongue. She possessed the remarkable ability to sew and fret at the same time.

"I am sure your ladyship has the kindest heart in the whole world, always helping some poor distressed soul. But I only hope that this time you don't end up arrested."

"Arrested? For what?"

"Abduction. It can't possibly be right to make off with someone else's legal ward."

"It's perfectly all right to prevent a poor innocent child from being forced into marriage with a man she's never laid eyes upon."

"Not a mere man, milady. He's said to be a very wealthy baronet."

"A baronet." Maria pulled a scornful face. "Some backwards country boor who has never once shown his face in town. He's probably quite fat, old, and wears doubtful linen."

"All the same, the Duke of Sheffield isn't going to like you meddling with his plans for his niece."

"I know." As far as Maria was concerned, His Grace's annoyance was only an added inducement.

"The duke's a proper villain, milady," Alice said with an eloquent shudder. "He quite terrifies me."

"Pooh! It's only the eye patch that makes him look so sinister. His Grace strikes me as the sort who enjoys bullying helpless females. I heartily dislike men of such stamp." A vision rose to Maria's mind, unwanted and involuntary, the image of her own father's stern face. But she immediately closed it out, as she did all unpleasant memories of her childhood, storing them away tighter than the diamonds she kept locked away in her jewel case.

She forced her mind back to what Alice was saying. ". . . and my late mistress never approved of the Duke of Sheffield either. Lady Butress always used to frown at His Grace and only give him a cold nod in passing."

"That certainly must have taught him a lesson," Maria said wryly. "I, however, prefer doing something a little more active to thwart His Grace's tyranny." Maria tapped one finger against the valentine. "Like helping Miss Lucas to arrange her escape."

"What sort of escape, milady?"

"Well, I don't exactly know yet," Maria admitted. "But rest assured, I will think of something very clever and—and daring."

"Oh dear. I hope this won't be like the time you arranged a match for Lady Clare, and her two suitors came to blows in the parlor. Or when you helped that young farm girl to elope and the coach overturned."

"Alice, I promise you. No coach wrecks. No fisticuffs," Maria soothed. "This time I will be very careful."

Maria held the valentine up to the light to examine her handiwork. The heart could not be proclaimed as good as new, but at least the inked words stood out clearly. Even Miss Selina Lucas should be able to figure out the time and place for the secret rendezvous. Miss Lucas was a sweet girl, although not very clever. But the code between her and Maria had been prearranged.

Now it only remained for Maria to find a way to slip the valentine to Miss Lucas without attracting the duke's attention. Sheffield was supposed to be the girl's guardian, but of late he had become more of a gaoler. Maria only hoped that Jared's nonsense had not lost for her the opportunity of getting the valentine to Miss Lucas before breakfast.

While Maria waited impatiently for the ink to dry, her maid lapsed into another lament. "I'm sure it's a noble thing you do, helping Miss Lucas and these other poor young females, but if only your lady-ship had someone to look out after you. What milady needs is a husband."

This was a familiar theme with Alice. She recommended a husband for Maria as often as she did doses of Dr. James's Powders.

"I already had a husband," Maria said.

"I mean you need a *good* one," Alice said, then blushed, adding hastily, "Er ... no, that is, I'm sure the late count was a very estimable man even if he was ... er, foreign. But milady is too young to remain a widow. You should think about another husband, a proper *English* one."

"My Roberto was worth ten of any Englishman." Maria glanced at the miniature she always carried with her. It stood propped on the dressing table, half-buried amidst a pile of her gloves. Maria had painted the portrait herself of Count Roberto di Montifiori Vincerone, and she was rather proud of her effort. She had succeeded in conveying the count's lean dark looks, the sleek mustache, the passion that fired his remarkable eyes. He was the image of all she'd ever dreamed of in a lover, tender, romantic, heroic.

"The count was so brave. And bold," Maria murmured, fingering the miniature's gilt rim. "He once rescued me from six Italian *banditti*."

"Six Italians?" Alice frowned, looking confused. "But I thought you said it was five Turks."

"That was another time," Maria said quickly. "When—when the Sultan of Tangier was trying to kidnap me for his harem."

"Goodness! What an adventurous life you have led, milady."

"Ye-e-es," Maria agreed, lowering her eyes. She wondered when she had gotten to be such a dreadful liar. But no, a soothing voice inside her asserted. She wasn't a *dreadful* liar. She was a remarkably accomplished one. Fiction was just another of her talents, like her ability to wield a paintbrush. And, she thought sadly, fiction sometimes could be so much more palatable than truth. She set the portrait away from her, relieved when Alice let the subject of husbands drop.

Maria had no intention of allowing her widowhood to end. She loved the independence that a handsome fortune gave her, and she was not about to surrender her freedom to the arbitrary whims and commands of some pompous English male. But she had to admit there were times, especially certain sleepless nights when she lay awake alone in her bed, that she did long for a pair of tender arms to hold her, a strong shoulder to nestle against.

Not a tyrannical husband, but a lover, a friend, a confidant, someone who would share her desire to right the injustices of the world, to help her plan such daring enterprises as the rescue of Miss Lucas.

A knight, a cavalier . . . a *hero*.

It was a curious and annoying thing that when such thoughts chased through her head, a face, a name, should persist in forcing its way into her mind.

Jared. Sir Jared Branden.

Maria scowled. She had no idea why she kept thinking of him, except for that fact that he had been plaguing her of late. But it was utter nonsense. She had given over the task of making a hero of Jared Branden a long time ago. Even if their acquaintance had begun with a daring rescue . . .

Her lips trembled into an unwilling smile at the remembrance. She'd gone out riding alone that hot July day. Just another futile attempt to impress her father, prove to him that he had sired more than a worthless girl.

Papa had always deplored her horsemanship, and his scorn had been complete when Maria had been too terrified to mount the large, restive mare he had purchased for her seventeenth birthday. She had then conceived the idiotic notion that Papa's instant love and approval could be won if only she could master the horse.

Slipping down to the stables, she'd had Lady Jane brought out. Her own groom would never have saddled the fractious horse for her, so Maria persuaded one of the stableboys to do so. Quaking in her boots, Maria had mounted the strapping cream-colored mare.

She managed to canter the horse out of the stable yard, but the temperamental Jane was already flattening back her ears. As they had crossed the meadow, Jane obeyed none of Maria's frantic commands.

By the time they reached the lane, the mare was doing her best to part company with her mistress. She bucked, twisted, and snapped. Heart thundering, Maria clutched at the reins, desperately seeking to maintain her precarious perch in the saddle.

Just then a curricle swept round the bend ahead of them, sending the mare into a full state of equine fury. Rearing back on her haunches, Jane attempted to slam Maria against the orchard fence. Maria yanked frantically at the reins, the world around her blurring in a dizzying rush of fear.

From a great distance, she heard a shout. Then *he* was there, looming up in front of the horse, a tall, stalwart young man, risking the danger of being knocked senseless by Jane's menacing hoofs.

Strong hands shot out, managing to gain a purchase on the mare's bridle. Before Maria could scarce comprehend what was happening, the horse had somehow gentled beneath her. In the next breath, Jane was being tied off to the fence post. And then those same strong hands were lifting Maria out of the saddle.

She didn't realize how terrified she had been until she felt the support of firm earth beneath her feet. She began to tremble so badly, her knees threatened to give way beneath her. She thought she would have sagged down but for her rescuer's firm grip upon her shoulders.

"Steady. Steady now," he murmured.

It was the same firm but gentle way he had talked to the horse, and Maria had to control an urge to burst into hysterical laughter. She took in deep gulps of air and managed to calm herself a little.

Then she dared glance at the face of her rescuer, and she found she could no longer breathe at all. It was as though every fantasy she'd ever dreamed in her lonely room back at the manor had suddenly sprung to life before her, every hero who'd ever carried her to safety from a burning building, every knight who'd swooped her up upon his charger, every chevalier who'd dueled to the death in her honor.

Jared's hair fell back in waves of glossy ebony, his eyes the hue of midnight, his jaw lean and strong, his mouth generous, sensitive. His shoulders, encased in a dashing driving cape, seemed broad enough to blot out the sun.

"Are you all right, miss?" he asked.

"Oh, yes," she managed to whisper.

"Not going to faint or anything, are you?"

She shook her head. It was just like in her dreams, all these tender inquiries. She stared deep into those thick-fringed dark eyes and waited for more.

"You little idiot!"

Maria blinked. "Wh-What?"

"I said, ma'am, you're an idiot."

Maria's brow furrowed. No, she couldn't have heard him right. None of the heroes in her dreams had ever said anything like that.

Jared released her and stepped back, scowling. "What did you think you were doing? A little slip of a girl like you trying to ride a strapping hulk of a horse like this one?"

"I'm not a slip of a girl," Maria said indignantly. She would have liked to draw herself up to her full height, but unfortunately she was already there and she barely reached his shoulder. "And my papa bought me that mare for my birthday."

"Humph! He must have been wishing it would be your last birthday then."

His flippant remark was so close to what Maria felt to be the truth, it was a moment before she could trust herself to answer him. She swallowed hard.

"My papa dotes upon me. If he thought that I'd been in the least danger, if that horse even so much as wheezed at me, it would be sold in a second."

"That would be a great mercy . . . for the horse."

"You are ungallant, sir."

"Ungallant? I just saved your pretty neck."

"Yes, but a true gentleman would be kinder. I would wager that no knight would ever have scolded a damsel in distress."

"Probably not, but I would have taught my damsel to manage her horse better and not wait around to be rescued. All that heavy armor, you know. I might not have been able to move fast enough to get there in time."

He was laughing at her now. Maria sniffed and regarded him with silent reproach.

He placed his hands on the flat planes of his hips. "What? Not a word of thanks for my daring rescue? Oh, I forget. You were *managing* before I came along."

He turned to Lady Jane, who was now nibbling at the tender shoots of a fruit tree just beyond the fence. Patting the horse's neck, he said, "Well, at least I'm sure you're grateful. I kept your mistress from sawing your mouth in half with that bit."

With her usual sweet disposition, Jane swung her head around and nipped savagely at his arm.

"Ow!" Jared exclaimed, drawing back, clutching his sleeve.

Maria suppressed a tiny smile, for the first time feeling in charity with her temperamental mount, especially when she saw that Lady Jane had succeeded in making a small rent in Jared's elegant driving cape.

He examined the damage and then muttered in accents of dark disgust. "Females!" Spinning on his heel, he started to stalk away.

Maria almost thought he meant to abandon her thus without another word. But he only stalked over to his curricle long enough to give his groom instructions about taking charge of that "ungrateful strumpet."

For one appalled moment, Maria wasn't certain whether Jared meant her or the horse. But the groom came forward to gather up Lady Jane's reins, and Jared beckoned for Maria to join him by the curricle.

She would have given all she possessed to have been able to tell the arrogant young man to drive on and leave her alone. But she dreaded the prospect of trying to ride Lady Jane again, knowing full well she couldn't even manage to lead the horse home.

She had no choice but to accept Jared's aide, no matter how ungraciously it was offered. Humbled by the all too familiar feeling of failure, the consciousness of her own inadequacies, Maria gathered what dignity she could muster.

She crossed over to the curricle, and Jared hoisted her onto the seat. His pair of showy bays stood docilely while he stalked back up the lane to retrieve his hat, which had flown off during the fracas.

It was then that Maria suffered a conscious pang, fearing perhaps she was the ungracious one. She hadn't noticed it before, but Jared had a dirty hoofprint on the front of his cape where he had been kicked. And his high-crown beaver hat had been entirely crushed in. Dear Lord, it could have been Jared's head.

Maria bit down upon her lip as Jared vaulted up onto the curricle seat beside her. She said in a small voice, "I'm sorry. You did rescue me, and you could have been killed doing so. You have my sincerest thanks."

Jared gathered up the reins of the curricle and angled a glance in her direction. "Your thanks? Given the condition of my brand-new hat, I'm not quite sure that's enough. You might offer me a reward."

"A—A reward?" she stammered in dismay. What sort of man was this? No true hero would have asked for such a thing. A true hero would be modestly disclaiming, declaring that risking his life for her was its own reward.

"I don't have my purse with me," she said. "But my home is just over that rise—"

He interrupted her with a laugh. "Your money would do me no good. The stuff slips through my fingers far too fast. No, I was thinking more of . . ."

Maria became aware of the way his bold dark eyes roved over her profile, his gaze seeming to fasten on her mouth.

"Didn't those damsels you spoke of usually offer their knights a kiss?"

Maria blushed hotly and squirmed. "I suppose sometimes they would let a knight kiss the hem of their gown."

Jared pulled a face. "The hem of your riding habit is dusty. But on the other hand," he murmured, "your mouth looks quite clean and very tempting."

"How dare you, sir." Maria inched farther away on the seat, but her heart had begun to pound faster.

"Very well." He sighed. "I suppose I do ask too much. I am likely a little delirious from the pain."

"Pain?"

He pressed one hand to his side. "It's nothing. Just a few glancing blows from your mare's hooves. I probably haven't really broken any ribs."

"Oh!" Maria cried.

He made an effort to straighten and suppressed a grimace. "It hardly seemed like too much to request one small kiss."

"But I couldn't possibly. I don't even know your name, sir."

"Jared. Jared Branden," he said, offering her his hand.

She slipped her fingers cautiously into his, and they seemed swallowed up in the strength of his grip.

"And you are?"

"Maria Addams, but—"

"Maria," he murmured, as though testing the sound of it on his tongue. "It's like music, just what a damsel in distress ought to be named. I like it."

He gave her a smile that flashed through her like a burst of sunlight. Still holding her hand, he bent his dark head closer. "And now that we have gone through the formality of introductions . . ."

"Oh, no," she breathed, her pulses skittering with panic. "I still can't possibly kiss—"

But his lips were already covering hers. The

panic that fluttered through her veins became a strange rush of excitement. She'd oft imagined what her first kiss would be like, so soft, pure, and chaste.

But Jared's mouth moved over hers in a way that was none of those things. It was a kiss that had stirred her blood, a kiss that had set her heart to thundering, a kiss that had shaken her out of her ivory tower and down to the Garden of Eden for a first forbidden taste of sweet, hot desire.

It was a kiss like . . . like so many other things about Jared Branden. Best forgotten.

Shivering, Maria dragged herself out of Jared's arms and back to the present, the somber surroundings of the guest bedchamber, Alice sewing quietly by the fire.

Maria pressed her hands to her cheeks, dismayed to feel the warmth flooding beneath her skin. It annoyed her to think that the memory of Jared's embrace should still have that power over her.

If she had to remember anything about the man, it shouldn't be his kisses, but the one fact that had stood out from the beginning of their acquaintance.

They were not suited to each other, had never been, she with all her romantic ideals, Jared with his cynical disregard for every tender emotion. They had bickered every time they met, disagreements that had stretched all the way through the fiery, temptestuous days of their brief courtship and engagement.

Disagreements that had finally come to a bitter end on a rainy day ten years ago. Jared had stirred the ashes of memory. Although she had not the least wish to do so, Maria couldn't help recalling how she had spent that long-ago Valentine's Day. In her bedchamber, her face pressed to the cold window, her silent tears tracking the course of the raindrops on the glass pane.

Even then she had had to fight the urge to run to the stables, fling herself on horseback, racing off to join Jared at the church. Hard, painful logic had prevailed and she had not stirred a step. But for long after that, she continued to have her doubts, continued to wonder what had held her back that day. Had it really been wisdom or only a lack of courage?

Maria sighed. As if any of that mattered now, of course. It was ancient history. She would never have given any of that unfortunate affair another thought if Jared hadn't turned up today to remind her.

And for all his teasing, she doubted that he gave the folly of their youth much consideration either. He had never been tender-hearted or nostalgic. No, he simply enjoyed plaguing Maria. It had always been the great mission of his life.

Now that he had had his bit of diversion with her this morning, she was unlikely to hear any more about their "anniversary." Whatever quirk of fate had brought Jared to Silversby on this particular day, Maria was certain he would not linger about when he discovered the earl's plans for the day.

A Valentine's ball and a supper to honor young love, the betrothal of the earl's youngest daughter. Maria could just see Jared grimace at the prospect. No, if she knew Jared Branden as well as she thought she did, she could predict with certainty what he was doing right now. Calling for his horse and preparing to ride like the devil, as fast and as far away from these romantic celebrations as he could get.

Chapter 3

After the warm welcome he'd received from Maria, Jared thought he was up to facing anything else the day might throw at him, even his uncle's displeasure. He supposed he owed his lordship an apology for arriving in such a condition last night. An inquiry of a servant revealed that his lordship awaited Mr. Branden in the study. Rapping at the door, Jared braced himself for a full salvo from his uncle's blistering tongue.

But the voice that bade him enter sounded odd, almost cheery. When Jared stepped into the book-lined study, he blinked. Lord Brixted generally kept the room as dour and somber as he had become himself in recent years, being troubled by the gout. But today the heavy curtains had been flung aside, flooding the room with winter sunlight. It was almost as blinding as the bottle green coat and striped waistcoat his lordship wore.

Bent over his desk, Lord Brixted brushed aside a few straggling ends of his salt-and-pepper hair. He looked up as Jared stepped into the room, his face creasing into such a beaming smile, Jared glanced behind him to see who else had entered.

"Ah, nevvy!" Lord Brixted shoved to his feet. "There you are at last."

Nevvy? Both of Jared's brows shot up. By God, the gout must have cleared up at last and the old man was back at the bottle again.

But Lord Brixted showed no signs of inebriation as he bustled round the desk and came forward to wring Jared's hand. He chortled. "Actually, I'm surprised to see you up and about so early, considering the state you were in last night, you young dog."

"Young dog?" Jared drawled. "The last time we met, I was that 'infernal cur.' It would seem I've risen a notch in your esteem."

"Now, now, sir." His uncle gave him a hearty clap on the shoulder. "Let's not cut up stiff over past differences."

"Heaven forfend. Especially since it appears you've been busy with cutting up of a different sort."

Jared leveled his quizzing glass at the litter-strewn desk, the remnants of a lace heart under construction. Turning brick red, his uncle hastened forward to sweep the valentine into a drawer.

Jared did his best to quell his amusement. He'd heard tell that Valentine's Day could have an odd effect on the most unlikely men. But Uncle Charles?

His lordship certainly was behaving strangely, spilling over with a bonhomie that included everyone, even his least favorite nephew. Before Jared knew where he was at, he was seated in the study's best leather armchair, being plied with his uncle's finest Madeira.

As Lord Brixted filled Jared's glass, he coughed

deprecatingly and said, "Of course, you must have noticed some changes about me."

"Indeed I have. Has the doctor been sent for?"

Even this quip failed to ruffle his lordship's good humor. "I was referring to my attire, man. What think you of my new coat?"

"It's very . . . green."

"It's cut after the latest fashion. The very thing to help a fellow appear dashing, my tailor assures me."

Perhaps it would have done, on a man thirty years younger, Jared thought. As his lordship paraded about for Jared's inspection, he caught an unmistakable creaking sound. Corsets, too?

"Er . . . you look very dapper, Uncle," Jared said. "What's the occasion?"

"It's Valentine's Day. Perhaps you may not have heard, but we're having a considerable celebration here today."

"Oh, yes, you're finally getting rid of— That is, I heard my fair cousin Caroline is to be betrothed."

That at least would account for some of this smiling humor, Jared thought. His avaricious uncle had probably succeeded in netting another man of fortune for one of his daughters.

"And who is the fortunate gentleman?" Jared asked, taking a swallow of his Madeira. "Some wealthy nabob, I trust?"

"No, actually, it's the Honorable Henry Tyne."

"Tyne? My dear uncle, you've slipped up this time," Jared mocked. "Tyne has barely four thousand a year."

"I know." For a brief moment his uncle scowled, then he rallied, saying, "But Caroline hasn't got the beauty of her sisters, and Tyne's worthy enough and . . . Oh, hellfire! It's a love match. I allowed Lady Montifiori Vincerone to persuade me to consent."

"Maria . . . You mean the contessa?"

His uncle nodded. "She's a very forceful woman."

"Slugged you, too, did she?" Jared murmured.

"What?"

"Nothing." Jared suppressed a smile. "I'm sure the contessa advised you well." He'd heard tell that Maria had become a noted matchmaker since her return to London society. So what had she been doing with that little valentine this morning? Finally working on a match for herself?

It still piqued Jared that he had no notion whom that valentine was for. He never could tolerate a mystery, he told himself. Sipping his wine, he wracked his brain for a subtle way to inquire what other male guests were staying at the manor. But before he could say another word, his uncle settled back behind the desk, excusing himself.

"I must crave your indulgence for a few minutes, Branden," he said. "Just a bit of business I must finish."

Jared shrugged and nodded. There was nothing now to prevent him taking his leave. But the impulse he'd had upon waking, to quit Silversby Manor as soon as possible, had left him.

Jared lounged back in his chair, no longer feeling in such a great hurry to be gone. Perhaps it was his surroundings. A good fire, a fine wine, an excellent library, had always been capable of rendering him mellow.

Stretching out his hand, he picked up a book that

had been left lying upon the tripod table at his elbow. He smiled slightly as he glanced at the spine, Chapman's translation of *The Odyssey*. Lord, he hadn't seen his own copy since he'd lent it to Maria when they had still been courting.

He'd been trying to convince the girl that other literature existed besides the faerie tales she had stuffed her pretty head with. For someone who doted upon his daughter as much as Maria's father was supposed to have done, the man had neglected his only child's education. Maria had been left amazingly ignorant, even for a woman. When he'd discovered this, Jared had set out for her a rigorous course of reading—

Jared's lips twisted. What a young cod's-head he had been. Courting a woman with books. Small wonder she'd jilted him. Sighing, he reshelved the book for his uncle, shelving bittersweet memories along with it.

Eventually becoming impatient with his uncle's silence, the busy *skritch* of his pen, Jared took a restless pace around the room. It was then he become aware of what the earl was doing, inking out words on small pieces of paper, sanding them dry, then folding and dropping the scraps into the depths of a low-crowned beaver hat.

"You'll pardon my asking, my lord," Jared said. "But what the devil are you doing?"

"Preparing for the lottery."

"Wouldn't you have a better chance of raising money if you just ran a faro table?"

"It's a Valentine's lottery, you young cawker. A romantic old custom."

"One that I appear to have remained mercifully unaware of."

"I put the names of all the gentlemen in the hat. The ladies do the choosing, and the couple matched up then become valentines," the earl explained. "Shall I toss in your name?"

"No, thank you," Jared said with an eloquent shudder. "I might be willing to hazard my neck, but not risk being paired with some hefty dowager with a booming voice."

"Neither am I." His uncle chuckled. "That's why I am not taking chances with my own name."

"What do you mean?"

His uncle held up one of the scraps. "I've dog-eared mine. Instead of allowing the ladies to do the drawing, I shall hand out the slips myself. That way I will be able to select my own name for the lady of my choosing. Clever, yes?"

"Oh, prodigiously," Jared said. Depend upon Uncle Charles to find a way to cheat. His honor, of course, had always required him to be aboveboard at cards, but his lordship never could be trusted at parlor games.

"And so what lady have you reserved for yourself, sir?"

To Jared's amusement and astonishment, his uncle blushed.

"What!" Jared rallied him. "Can it be Cupid has already made you his mark?"

Lord Brixted tugged at his neckcloth and said, "Well, you might have noticed I have been a widower a long time now."

"No! I wondered where my aunt had got to."

"This is not a matter for jest, sir. I suppose you regard me as too old to think of courting again."

"Not at all. Who is the fortunate lady and when am I to wish you joy?"

"No need to be quite that precipitate, but there is one of my guests that has, shall we say, excited my admiration. A charming and beautiful lady . . . the contessa."

Jared had been in the act of raising his glass to his lips, but he paused. "The contessa?"

"Aye. Any woman who'd run off and marry an Italian count, I expected to be something of a fool. But no such thing. Maria's quite remarkable."

"I suppose she is," Jared said slowly. He tossed down the rest of his Madeira, no longer finding his uncle quite so amusing.

"I hear that her first husband left her well off, very well off indeed." The earl smacked his lips, whether over the wine, Maria, or the size of her fortune, Jared couldn't be sure. But his uncle wouldn't be the first man Jared had ever heard speculating over the size of Maria's inheritance.

He remembered at White's one evening, Mr. Brisbain, a noted fortune hunter, going on and on about "the pretty rich little widow," bandying Maria's name about, boasting about the prospect of coupling her charms and her bank account.

Boring fellow, Brisbain, Jared thought with a scowl. He had occasion to knock the yellow-haired fop down the stairs later that same night, though Jared couldn't recollect precisely what Brisbain had done to annoy him. Likely it had been the color of his coat. Jared couldn't abide the color green when he was in his cups.

Perhaps he didn't like it much when he was so-
ber either. His jaw tightening, Jared stared at his
uncle, the old fool's portly frame encased in that absurdly youthful coat.

His lordship continued to expound upon Maria's
charms. ". . . and besides the villa in Italy, there's
an estate in Norfolk, to say nothing of an income
rumored to be above twenty thousand a year. We'd
be a perfect match. I daresay a sensible woman like
Maria would enjoy acquiring a title."

"She already has one."

"Oh, that Italian nonsense doesn't count. If she
married me, she'd be a real countess." His lordship
shook with a sudden chuckle. "That would be quite
a jest on you, m'boy, wouldn't it? Having to call
such a pretty young thing 'auntie.' "

"Indeed it would. Far more than you could possibly imagine," Jared murmured. Few members of
his distant family had ever known of his brief engagement to Maria. It might be a little awkward
revealing such a thing to his uncle now. Also unnecessary.

Maria was far too much the romantic to ever consider wedding for the sake of a title, especially a
gout-ridden man nearly twice her age. Wasn't she?

"Far be it from me to discourage all these roman-
tic visions, Uncle," Jared said with forced lightness.
"But perhaps the contessa has already laid some
Valentine's plans of her own."

"Nothing that I can't sweep aside. You forget I
was accounted something of a rake in my day. I
still know how to get round any woman." The earl
leered and shot Jared a conspiratorial wink.

Jared felt his hand tense around his wineglass. It

was fortunate perhaps that at that moment they were interrupted. The butler stepped inside to announce that the Reverend Jameson had come to call, and in a state of great distress.

"Tiresome fellow," the earl growled. "Probably come to complain about my hunt going through the churchyard, knocking over some of the gravestones again."

"Unreasonable man," Jared said, but his irony was lost on the earl, who solemnly agreed.

"I shall have to go deal with him, I suppose. Clergymen are always a plagued nuisance. Amuse yourself until I return, Branden," the earl commanded.

Long after the door had closed behind his uncle, Jared stood contemplating his lordship's schemes regarding Maria. Poor Maria, with that little paper heart she'd worked so hard upon, no doubt dreaming of her mysterious "hero, bold and true." Jared pulled a sour face.

After that clout she'd given Jared, it would serve her right to end up with Lord Brixted. Instead of whatever romantic plans she'd imagined, she'd spend her Valentine's Day fending off the advances of an elderly roué. Well, she wasn't a green girl any longer. She certainly could look out for herself.

But as he turned to go, Jared felt pulled back. He stared down into the contents of that silk-lined hat, until he felt one of his devilish impulses coming over him.

"Ah, Branden, Branden!" Jared clucked his tongue at himself. "You're getting far too old for these pranks."

But he rummaged inside the hat, fishing out the

dog-eared slip of paper that bore Lord Brixted's name. His uncle would be furious, of course. But then it was his lordship's own fault. He should never have ordered Jared to amuse himself. His lips curving into an unholy smile, Jared reached for a pen and ink.

Gathering up the train of her ball gown, the shimmering folds of lilac silk rustling about her ankles, Maria crept towards the drawing room. It was absurd, but she had been tiptoeing around all day, half expecting Branden to pounce upon her again. But there had been no sign of the man, not even at tea, and Jared had never been one to miss a meal.

It must be as she had supposed. He had ridden off again. Of course, she was relieved, but Jared had already done his damage. He had prevented her from encountering Miss Lucas before breakfast, and the girl had been closeted in her room most of the afternoon.

Now Maria was faced with the far riskier prospect of attempting to pass the valentine off to Miss Lucas during the ball itself, under the Duke of Sheffield's very nose. The paper heart was folded and tucked inside Maria's reticule. She was as conscious of its presence as any spy carrying secret documents.

But as she made her entrance into the drawing room, she felt that her luck had turned. Miss Lucas was sitting alone by the long windows, gazing out at the night with a melancholy air. For once, she seemed to have escaped her dragon's watchful eye.

Maria headed in the girl's direction only to be intercepted by her host. The Earl of Brixted bowed deeply over her hand, paying her many effusive compliments, his eyes trying to dip down places in her gown where they had no business going.

"I'm so glad you came down early, my dear. Before the other guests arrive from the neighborhood, I've arranged a little surprise for the company."

"Oh, dear," Maria murmured. "I'm not sure I'm up for any more surprises today."

She whisked her hand away as the earl was about to carry it to his lips, leaving him kissing air. Excusing herself, she made her way to Miss Lucas's side.

The girl glanced with a wan smile at Maria's approach. She had a delicate, heart-shaped face framed by glossy chestnut tresses. Never had any young lady looked more designed for the role of persecuted heroine. Her mouth had a tragical droop. Her large, lustrous brown eyes could have melted the heart of any man. Except Sheffield. The bastard had none.

"Good evening, child," Maria said. "How are you?"

Miss Lucas's lips trembled. But she gave a brave little sigh. "As well as one might expect, Countess. Thank you."

"Were you ill this afternoon? You did not even come down for tea."

"My uncle thought it best I spend my time resting."

"Resting? That is as novel a description for imprisonment as I have ever heard."

"Oh, Countess. Please!" Miss Lucas cast an agonized glance around her as though fearful of being overheard.

49

Maria gave her gloved hand a comforting squeeze. "Courage, my dear. You shall have a message of comfort soon from someone deeply interested in your welfare."

She started to undo her reticule to pull out the valentine when Miss Lucas exclaimed in terror, "Oh, no! No messages. You know His Grace reads everything."

"That is why we established the code," Maria reminded her in low tones.

"Code?"

"Yes, our secret code."

"Oh, dear," Miss Lucas faltered. "I'm afraid I've forgotten it."

Maria stifled an impatient exclamation. She started to whisper the code again, but it was both hopeless and ridiculous. She might as well give Miss Lucas the message directly and be done with it. The girl obviously had a great deal to learn about conducting an intrigue.

"Now, let me see." Miss Lucas's smooth brow knit in a puzzled frown. "I go through the words and pick out every fourth letter and turn them around backwards. Or is it every fifth?"

"Never mind about the letters," Maria began when she was interrupted by an icy voice.

"Someone is missing some letters?"

Maria did not even have to turn around to know who stood behind her. Miss Lucas's face said it all. The girl had turned as white and quivery as a blancmange.

Maria came slowly about to make her curtsy to His Grace of Sheffield. The duke was not a large man, not much taller than Maria, in point of fact.

But somehow His Grace had learned to cast a long shadow.

He preferred the styles of the previous generation, his coat of black brocade trimmed with silver lacing only adding to his sinister aura. A gray powdered wig concealed a pate left bald by smallpox, but little could be done to disguise the ravages to his face. The eye that had been deformed by the disease was covered with a black patch. All the duke's malevolence centered in his remaining good eye, which glittered coldly at Maria.

She shivered in spite of herself.

"What is this about letters?" he repeated.

"Your Grace misheard me. One of the hazards of eavesdropping," Maria said smoothly. "I was only asking your niece if she was feeling better."

"How good of you to inquire, my lady" He gave a thin smile. "Always so concerned, so busy on behalf of others."

"I—I told her I was quite well, Uncle," Miss Lucas faltered.

"I wish I could say the same for the countess." Sheffield fixed Maria with his gaze. "You look so pale, madam. I am becoming deeply concerned for your health."

"Are you indeed?" Maria asked tartly.

"There seems to be a chill in this part of the room. Dangerous things, chills. You might be well advised to move away from my niece and go sit near the fire."

The suggestion was voiced in the softest of accents, but there was no mistaking the undertone of warning. Maria's pulse gave an uneasy flutter, but she refused to budge. She would not allow herself to be disconcerted by His Grace of Sheffield.

Only one man had ever been able to do that and—

Maria's heart sank. And that man had just entered the room, his limp doing little to take the swagger out of his step.

Branden.

He had not gone away after all, and she had been foolish to presume that he would. If there was one thing that could be depended upon with Jared, it was that he was thoroughly unpredictable.

Candlelight shone on his dark hair, as black and glossy as a raven's wing, the thick mane brushed back with the same raffish carelessness with which he arranged his snowy white cravat. He smiled and bowed to the various guests as though attending Valentine's soirees were the delight of his life.

"Well, Branden!" Lord Brixted exclaimed. "You decided to join the festivities after all."

"How could I miss such a spectacular event?"

"I don't know about spectacular," the earl said modestly. "Just a little music, a little dancing, the sort of thing to please the ladies."

"Will there be any prizefighting?"

"Of course not. Ladies don't like that sort of thing."

"I don't know." Jared angled a wicked glance at Maria. "Obviously you haven't consulted the tastes of all your guests."

No one could possibly have understood Jared's jest except for herself, but several of the young ladies tittered anyway. Maria felt her face grow hot and deliberately turned her back.

To her dismay, she discovered Sheffield had used the distraction of Jared's arrival to whisk Miss Lucas away. He now had the girl across the room on the settee, wedged between the dowager Lady Lakemore and the spinsterish Miss Tandy.

Once more Maria saw her opportunity was lost. Disgruntled, she sank into the seat Miss Lucas had vacated. She couldn't entirely blame Jared for this, but she did. Damn the man! He couldn't be in a room for two minutes without managing to fluster her.

At least he had the prudence to keep his distance. While Lord Brixted produced a hat, organizing some sort of parlor game, Jared folded his arms, lounging in the corner by the fireplace. It should have been easy to ignore him, but it wasn't.

Maria doubted that any female in the room who was still breathing could have done so. Jared was the sort of man who seemed born to look good in the formal attire of black evening wear. The severe tailoring, the touch of lace on his cravat, only seemed to accent his aura of masculinity. It annoyed Maria no end that she should still be obliged to acknowledge Jared's attractiveness.

Time had deepened the lines of his countenance, turning a smooth-faced young man into something more hard-edged, dangerous. The full, sensual curve of Jared's lips hinted that he, too, had acquired secrets over the years, secrets that were probably more sinfully exciting and interesting than hers.

Even his wartime injury had done him no disservice. His body was still that of a lean, well-honed athlete, his limp only putting her in mind of fierce, dark-haired warriors of yore, battle-scarred heroes who—

No, Maria checked the foolish thought. Battle-scarred heroes didn't wield quizzing glasses, which was what Branden was doing now. He was training his at her, subjecting her frame to a warm, lingering perusal that caused her blood to thrum through her veins.

She wondered irritably when he had adopted such a dandified affectation. He never used to employ a quizzing glass, had never needed one to stare her out of countenance, to melt right through the ice of her dignity.

She remembered the next time she had seen him after their first disastrous encounter in the lane. Papa must have begun to fear that he would have Maria left on his hands forever, because he finally had been persuaded to let her attend her first public dance.

He'd dispatched her to the local assembly in the care of his cousin, a wretched arrangement. Mrs. Henderson had two daughters of her own to partner off, and she did not regard Maria as a welcome addition to the party.

For most of the evening she left Maria to the comforts of tepid punch and counting the flowers on the wallpaper. Papa had never permitted Maria to get to know the other young people of the neighborhood. Feeling shy and alone, Maria attempted to disguise her misery behind a mask of disdain, affecting to scorn her surroundings. She might have carried it off, but he had been there.

Jared Branden, that arrogant young man who had escorted her home after her riding disaster, kissed her senseless, then dumped her unceremoniously in the stable yard with the advice to trade her mare in for a pony. Jared was not from one of the local families, only visiting in the neighborhood, so she'd cherished the fervent hope she'd never have to see him again. And surely after another two weeks had passed, he'd also have the decency to stop haunting her dreams.

But the sets were forming for the next dance, and here he was, that infernal wicked man, moving slowly but inexorably in her direction.

Maria stiffened, staring ahead of her with as much hauteur as she could muster. It made no difference. He simply stepped directly in front of her so that she could see no one, nothing but him.

"Good evening, Titania."

She had not intended to speak to him, but it was impossible to ignore such a greeting.

"That is not my name," she said indignantly.

"It's from *Midsummer Night's Dream*. Shakespeare."

"Of course. Everyone knows that." Everyone but her. She had no more knowledge of Shakespeare than the kitchen cat. Papa had never allowed her to attend a play.

"Titania," Jared murmured. "The proud queen of faeries. Disdainful, but beautiful. It suits you."

"The other day you said Maria suited me," she began, then halted in dismay. She hadn't meant to bring up what had happened the other day at all. It was too rife with warm, dangerous memories that all seemed to center in the wicked, tempting curve of Jared's mouth.

"We shouldn't be discussing my name at all," she

concluded primly. "We have never been properly introduced."

"Oh, that's easily taken care of."

To her mortification, Jared turned and snared a moon-faced gentleman who was attempting to maneuver back through the crowd with a glass of punch for his dancing partner.

"Good evening, sir. How do you do?" Jared said. "Jared Branden's the name."

The gentleman looked dumbfounded at being addressed by a total stranger, but he stammered politely, "P-Pleased to make your acquaintance."

"And that young lady is Miss Maria Addams. Do you not find her very beautiful?"

Maria stifled a groan and looked about for a chair large enough to crawl beneath.

"Oh. Oh, yes, she's quite lovely," the obliging gentleman replied.

"Good. Then introduce us."

"What?"

"Be so good as to present me to the young lady," Jared prodded.

The gentleman rolled his eyes, looking as though he feared he was dealing with a madman. He bowed to Maria, who resisted the urge to bury her face in her hands.

"Miss Addams, may I present to you Mr. Jarvis—"

"No, that's Jared," Jared hissed in a stage whisper.

"Mr.—Mr. Gerald Branden."

"Close enough. Thank you, sir." He clapped the bewildered man on the shoulder and permitted him to go on his way. The gentleman heaved an audible sigh of relief as he escaped.

"There." Jared turned triumphantly back to Maria. "Now we have been properly introduced."

Maria tried to maintain a stern facade, but it was impossible. She pressed one gloved hand to her lips to stifle the laughter that welled inside of her. "You are perfectly abominable, sir."

"Yes, I suppose I am. But you should have thought of that before you sought out my acquaintance. At least now that we are introduced, you will be able to dance the next set with me."

"Is that what this is all about, sir?" Maria asked, peering coyly above the rim of her fan. "You wished to dance with me?"

"No, not in the least."

"Oh." She lowered the fan, humiliated by his blunt reply.

"It's nothing personal, Titania," he said. "I merely hate dancing. But it is the only way at an assembly that I can spend time in your company, and that, I assure you, is something I want more than anything else in the world."

"Oh," was all she could think of to say again. She had never known anyone capable of putting her through such a dizzying rush of emotions, hurt indignation to a state of warm breathlessness.

He offered her his arm, and she took it before she half realized what she was doing. He led her to the bottom of the last set.

As they stepped into the opening movements of the dance, he said, "These infernal dances last far too long, but at least it gives me the opportunity to talk to you."

"I can't imagine what we have to talk about, sir," she murmured.

"You can start by telling me how many flowers were on the wall."

"What?"

"You were counting them, weren't you?"

It mortified her that he should have noticed her partnerless state. They were separated by the movement of the dance. But by the time they came together again, she rallied enough to say, "Five hundred and seventy-four."

"I beg your pardon."

"There are five hundred and seventy-four flowers."

He flashed her that smile that was like lightning.

"Now we have nothing left to converse about, sir."

"No fear of that, Miss Addams. I can always think of something to say. That's what frequently gets me into so much trouble."

But for a young gentleman who boasted of being so loquacious, Jared remained silent. He gave the impression not of a man who wouldn't talk, but of one who was simply forgetting to do so.

He spoke instead with his eyes. His gaze followed her every movement, and when they were separated, it was his eyes that seemed to draw her back to his side.

Their hands met as they circled in a slow, languorous rhythm, and she had the curious sensation of at once floating and sinking down, deeper and deeper into the dark pools of his eyes.

"I'm glad we met again," she said. "I wanted to correct the mistaken impression you must have of me. Out riding alone unchaperoned, without even my groom. You must have received the impression that I am very fast."

He chuckled at that. "The horse was fast. You, my charming Maria, are rather slow. I have a feeling that was the first time you ever indulged in a stolen kiss."

Her cheeks burned. "It wasn't right for you to kiss me. You couldn't have thought me a proper lady."

"Oh, the properest."

"But it's an insult for a gentleman to kiss a well-bred young lady. Why didn't you apologize?"

"If I were to say I was sorry I kissed you, that would be an even worse insult, Titania."

"But it still wasn't right."

"It felt incredibly right to me," he said with a look that set her heart to pounding. "But I will contrive to behave like a gentleman if that is what you wish. I won't kiss you again until we are formally betrothed."

"Betrothed!" He startled her so that she missed her footing. He had to guide her until she found her place back in the dance.

"You shouldn't jest about such things," she said reproachfully.

"I wasn't jesting." The tone of his voice left no room for doubt, no more than did the sudden fire and intensity in his remarkable dark eyes.

"You couldn't possibly know that you wish to marry me after only two meetings," she protested.

"I knew the first time I looked into your eyes, Titania."

"So what do you think of that, Contessa?"

"I think it's the most insane thing I've ever heard."

"You do?"

The voice that questioned her was too gruff to be Jared's. Maria blinked, aware of an awkward silence descending around her. She wrenched herself back through time, back from her memories of the assembly hall to the reality of the Earl of Brixted's drawing room.

A drawing room in which everyone was staring at her. Even Jared regarded her questioningly. Maria forced a weak, apologetic smile to her lips, embarrassed to realize she'd been doing it again. Spinning off onto some nostalgic reverie like an old woman daydreaming in her armchair. Dear God, and she wasn't even thirty yet.

Maria glanced up to find Lord Brixted hovering before her, a curly-brimmed hat in his hand.

"I am sorry, my lord," she said. "I fear I didn't comprehend your question."

"I said it was finally your turn. Now, what do you think of that?"

"My turn?"

"To receive a name in our lottery, the name of the gentleman who will be your valentine."

Oh, that was what this nonsense was all about. Seeing some slips in the bottom of the hat, Maria gave a tiny shrug of resignation and started to reach for one.

But the earl drew back almost coyly and wagged an admonishing finger at her. "Now, Contessa, you must play fair, as all the other ladies did. I am being Cupid tonight. I will select the name and hand it to you."

The earl held up one hand, dove his fingers into the hat, and made a great show of feeling about for one of the slips. He produced the paper with a grand flourish. There was a breathless hush as the earl slowly presented the folded slip to Maria, clearly enjoying the suspense he created.

Only Jared appeared unmoved. He leaned against the mantel, regarding his fingernails in a posture of indifference. But beneath the calm facade, he waited with a tension that would have rivaled Guy Fawkes's anticipation of the blowing up of Parliament.

Except unlike Fawkes, Jared was more sure of his explosion.

Maria unfolded the paper and began to read aloud.

"Sir Jared . . ." Her voice faded to a horrified whisper. "Branden."

"What!" Lord Brixted bellowed. "That's not possible. I—I mean, let me see that." He snatched the paper from Maria's fingers.

Jared decided it was time to make his move. Straightening slowly, he crossed to his uncle's side and peered over his uncle's shoulder.

"Dear me, the contessa has drawn my name. How very fortunate. I haven't been so lucky on other Valentine's Days. How glad I am I decided to stay."

The shock slowly wearing off, both Maria and his uncle looked daggers at him. Color suffused into their faces, the only difference being that while Maria had turned a most becoming shade of valentine pink, Lord Brixted waxed an alarming hue of purple.

Chapter 4

He'd already managed to lose his valentine, Jared thought with a wry crook of his lips. Or rather, she was avoiding him. Maria circulated about the drawing room, conversing lightly with the other guests. She reminded Jared of a restive mare he'd once owned. Every time she saw him approaching with the harness, she'd bolt to another corner of the pasture. There'd only been one way to coax that filly to bridle.

But Jared doubted holding out a peace offering of sugar cubes would work with Maria. She'd likely bite his hand off instead. So he held back, biding his time. The night was young. The local guests whom his uncle had deemed worthy of an invitation to the manor were still arriving, and the musicians were just setting up in the alcove.

Sooner or later Maria would be obliged to speak to him, but until then, Jared remained content to admire her from a distance. The lilac silk gown she wore, with its rich trim and sweeping train, was worthy of an empress. As was the diamond pendant that glittered cold against the creamy swell of her décolletage. Her blond hair was piled high atop her head, drawing attention to the graceful curve of her neck.

She looked utterly magnificent, and yet he preferred her as she'd been that morning, in simple white muslin, her only adornment the soft fall of her faerie gold curls, the only adornment she'd ever needed, his Titania.

He supposed Maria had finally become all she'd ever desired, an elegant creation of charm and sophistication, quite the grand lady. He rather missed the shy, dreamy-eyed girl she'd once been, but there was no denying the allure of the woman before him. It was a remarkable transformation from that self-conscious little miss to this radiant, goddesslike female. A transformation in which he had played no part.

The thought left him feeling rather melancholy, but that was a mood that Jared did not tolerate. Before he allowed himself to become blue-deviled, far better to cross the room and devil her.

He managed to corral Maria as she was deep in conversation with Mr. Henry Tyne, a golden-haired young man with such a fresh-scrubbed appearance that Jared was always tempted to check and see if he was still wet behind the ears.

Tyne appeared to be boring on forever about the perfections of his intended, Jared's cousin Caroline, and Maria was actually encouraging him. But at Jared's approach, Tyne bowed and said, "Now, if you will excuse me, I must go and find my angel. No man must claim her for the first dance but me."

With a beatific look on his face, Tyne wandered off. Jared shook his head and demanded of Maria,

"Good Lord! Did I behave like such a mooncalf when I was betrothed to you?"

The smile that Maria had been bestowing on Mr. Tyne vanished. The only reply Jared received to his question was an arctic look.

Jared rubbed his arms and shivered. "Brr. Did some fool throw open a window? The air in this corner of the room is positively frigid."

Maria heaved a long-suffering sigh. "Why are you doing this, Branden?"

"Doing what?"

"Persecuting me this way. Is this some sort of well-plotted revenge you are executing because I jilted you ten years ago?"

"My dear girl, I have no idea what you mean. What an absurdly melodramatic notion."

"You know exactly what I mean. This can't be coincidence, your arriving unexpected at Silversby Manor. Then, of all the gentlemen here, I end up with your name as my valentine."

"It was Lord Brixted who did the lottery. How could I possibly have rigged it so you would get my name?"

"I don't know. But I'm certain you did. You would go to any lengths to torment me."

"You give me credit for a deal more energy than I possess. I know I have many faults, Maria, but when it came to that lottery, I played the game with as much fairness and honesty as my own uncle."

Maria frowned. Something about Jared's protestations of innocence did not ring true, but the more she thought about it, her accusation did sound ridiculous. Even if Jared could have manipulated the lottery, would he really put himself to the trouble of doing so? Would he still think her important enough to waste such effort? Such imaginings smacked of unpardonable vanity on her part.

"I'm sorry," she finally said. "Perhaps I have accused you unjustly."

"That's all right. I forgive you, in the spirit of the day. After all, you are my valentine."

"Oh, no. We may have been tossed together again by some malicious whim of fate, but you need not feel obliged to carry this nonsense any further."

"Indeed I do," he said, his dark eyes dancing. "You see, I have been studying up on this old custom of the valentine lottery. In some parts of the world, if the gentleman abandons the lady who has chosen him, she has the right to burn him in effigy."

"I already burned yours a long time ago," she said sweetly, and attempted to move past him. But Jared caught her arm, his fingers encircling her wrist.

"Maria," he murmured. "Surely after all this time, we are both grown-up enough to set our differences aside. No one takes this valentine nonsense seriously. We could at least act like old friends for one evening."

"I don't recall a time when we were ever 'friends.'"

"That's why it would be such a novelty. Please?"

Jared was never more dangerous than when he infused that low, coaxing note into his voice. After all these years, one would think she would be proof against it. Although she drew her hand away, Maria felt herself relenting.

"Well, the musicians appear ready to strike up. I suppose as my chosen valentine, I should at least favor you with the first dance."

"That would be an interesting favor indeed. But you might have better luck standing up with a broomstick. It would be far more graceful." A rare bitterness sounded beneath Jared's attempt to jest.

Maria was at a loss to understand it until, horrified, she remembered. His leg.

"Oh, Jared, I—I am so sorry," she cried. "I wasn't thinking—"

"It's all right, my dear," he interrupted with a grimace. "You know I always hated dancing anyway."

"I'm not that fond of it myself anymore," she said. "Perhaps we could just sit and—and here, let me get you a chair."

The taut set of his mouth relaxed into his usual air of amusement. "I'm not an invalid, Maria. Though, of course, I have no objection to being fussed over by a beautiful woman. But why don't you do your fussing over here?"

Linking his arm through hers, he steered her over to an area by the tall, latticed windows that overlooked the snow-covered gardens. Maria slowed her pace, suddenly more conscious of his halting step than she had been before. As Jared lowered himself beside her on the ottoman sofa, she did indeed have to curb an urge to fuss, offer him help that clearly wasn't needed or wanted.

Jared had obviously grown used to coping with his injury. This tender solicitude she felt towards him was absurd, absurd as the nervous fluttering she was experiencing. During the few times she had encountered Jared since her return from abroad, they had met only in passing at a ball or the theater. Such meetings had followed the invariable routine of a duel, a feint from him, a parry from her.

But if they truly were going to lower their swords this time, she wasn't sure if she knew how to behave. Unfurling her fan, she waved it briskly, pretending great interest in the line of dancers forming for the first set.

"Who's the chit with young Tyne?" Jared asked.

"Why, it's Caroline. Don't you recognize your own cousin?"

"It's been a while since I've seen her. But I suppose I might have guessed who she was, if nothing else than from that dazed look on her face. It matches his."

"They are very much in love, sir."

"And greatly indebted to you, so I understand. I hear you persuaded my uncle to give his consent to the match. However did you manage it?"

"It's simply a question of understanding Lord Brixted. He is most mellow when he's in the saddle. I went out riding with him two days ago. When my teeth finally stopped chattering from the cold, I pleaded Mr. Tyne's suit. I was able to convince your uncle somewhere between our gallop across the meadow and when we jumped the hedge."

Jared angled her a look of pure astonishment. "You jump now?"

Maria gave a rueful smile. "No, but the horse his lordship loaned me did, and I was obliged to be amiable and go along. Your uncle was lost in admiration of my form. I daresay he'd never seen a woman take a leap leaning half out of the saddle, clinging to the reins with her teeth."

Her laughter mingled with his, and some of the constraint between them seemed to dissolve. Jared shook his head, a wondering light in his eyes.

"Can it be you have finally developed a sense of humor, Contessa? You were always wont to take yourself so seriously. As I recall, you used to be remarkably sensitive about your equestrian skills."

If she had become less sensitive, Maria supposed it was owing to the fact that she no longer had to face her father's scorn. But to Jared she said, "Some things leave one little choice but to laugh. My horsemanship has always been one of those. But what of you? I suppose you are still mad for—" Maria broke off as she caught herself on the brink of another horrible blunder. She glanced self-consciously to the leg Jared kept stretched out rather stiffly before him. "I'm sorry. Of course, you don't ride anymore. I'm sure you're too busy with—with other diversions."

"Oh, yes, I have a fat little pony that I trot out on now and then." He grinned at her. "Of course I still ride, you goose, only with not quite the same dash." He heaved a mock sigh. "I'm getting a little too old to be that reckless anymore."

"Quite in your dotage, in fact," she retorted, eyeing the unblemished darkness of his hair, the character lines that only added to the roguish attractiveness of his face.

"Time has dealt far more kindly with you," she complained. "But it is always thus with men. It is most unfair."

He caught hold of one of her hands. "Oh, no, Titania," he said, raising her gloved fingertips to his lips. "It is you who is very much the faerie princess you were at eighteen, only perhaps a shade more regal." His gaze dropped to her décolletage, his eyes warming with frank admiration.

"In fact, much more regal in certain respects," he said wickedly.

Maria gasped and dealt him a sharp rap with her fan. The outrageous remark was so like Jared. But she had to turn aside to hide a tiny smile. She'd always been such a scrawny girl. It foolishly pleased her that Jared should have noticed she had finally filled out.

She took refuge behind her fan before making a confession that was likely unwise, but she could not seem to help herself.

"Even though I was living in Italy, I had the London papers sent to me. I followed the accounts of how our army was doing in Spain. I couldn't help noticing your name, the detailing of your heroic actions. Small wonder that you were knighted."

"Oh, indeed," Jared drawled. "They've got to hand those knighthoods out to somebody."

"But you were magnificent. Your regiment was in flight, total panic, when you saved the day, rallied your troops for one final desperate charge into the jaws of death itself."

Maria hated to admit how often she had looked for Jared's name. It had surprised her to see him mentioned at all in the dispatches. The Branden family had a strong military tradition. Both Jared's older brothers and his younger one had all taken commissions. But Jared had always scorned the army, saying that if he wanted to set himself up for a target, he could do so just as comfortably at home by going grouse hunting with his grandfather, who was nearsighted.

Yet something appeared to have changed his mind in the year after Maria had left England, for the name of one Lieutenant Jared Branden began to appear often in the *Post*. The account of his last heroic action had been so glorious, Maria had imagined the scene many times. Jared, with the sweat of battle glistening upon his soot-streaked face, his eyes fierce as he urged his magnificent black charger forward. Saber drawn, he single-handedly slew at least a dozen villainous Frenchmen, until the terrifying explosion of the cannon. Jared fell from the saddle, blood soaking his pant leg. His teeth clenched heroically, he tried to fight on, only to sag back, overcome with an agony few mortals could have endured.

The thought of it was still enough to bring a lump to her throat—that is, until Jared's voice cut through this noble vision with his usual amused mockery.

"My dear Maria, I don't know what you read, but what actually happened was this. With all that smoke, I got turned around and headed the wrong way. For some reason, the rest of the idiots followed me. No sane man would charge headlong into the enemy's cannon fire on purpose."

Maria didn't believe him for a moment. It had always been one of Jared's annoying traits. Whenever she had attempted to set him up on a pedestal, he had ruthlessly toppled it, forever disclaiming any noble intentions, turning the most heroic of his actions into a jest.

"You are just being modest," she insisted. "Deny it how you will, I know you must have been very brave that day. You were hideously wounded."

"That much is true. It was a great nuisance having such a large hole blown in my best uniform trousers. It took so long for any help to get through to the wounded, I was certain I was a dead man. Only one thought kept me going, kept me struggling to survive."

"What was that?" Maria asked softly.

He looked at her, his eyes blazing with an intensity that left her breathless. Then he appeared to give himself a sharp mental shake.

"Why, the thought of looters coming through, pillaging my body." Jared gave a comical grimace. "I heard tell that they'd even steal your teeth."

"Oh." She stiffened, averting her profile.

His answer had clearly disappointed her, and he wondered why he'd done that, why, for once, he couldn't have told her the truth. That what had kept him alive on that grim and awful day had been one word, a name that he'd kept repeating over and over again like a prayer, a litany.

Maria. He'd held the pain at bay by conjuring up her face, his lady of the flaxen hair, his faerie-eyed maiden of the impossible dreams. She'd left him, but as long as she continued to inhabit some corner of this earth, he knew that he would always want to live.

But what a clunch he would sound if he confessed such nonsense to her now. Besides, he hadn't even known what he'd been saying. He'd been delirious, out of his mind with pain.

No, it was far easier to settle himself back

against the window in a negligent pose and tease her. "What's the matter, Titania? Still searching for a hero? I thought you'd found him in your Count Vincent Macaroni."

She bridled immediately at that. "His name was Roberto di Montifiori Vincerone, from a very old and aristocratic Italian family."

"Like the Borgias?"

"No!" She vented her displeasure by dealing him another sharp rap with her fan.

Rubbing his knuckles, Jared made haste to apologize. "Sorry. I'm sure that your Count Roberto was a noble specimen. I've heard the rumors that his death came as a great shock, very untimely and tragic."

"Yes, he—he fell off of an Alp."

There was a pregnant pause. Jared tried to keep a straight face. But some of his irreverent thoughts must have been visible, for Maria added fiercely, "Not an Italian Alp. A French one."

"Ah, that explains everything. Always treacherous, those French."

"I might have known you would poke fun. It's not amusing." Turning her back to him, Maria rummaged through her reticule for her handkerchief, which she held to her face.

After an awkward silence, Jared rested one hand upon her shoulder and said, "I'm sorry, Maria."

He was sorrier still to discover she was still grieving for that man. He longed to groan aloud, *How could you leave me at the church door, then run off to the continent and marry some Italian with a preposterous name and not even enough sense to keep his feet on solid ground?*

How did a fellow go about killing himself by tumbling off a mountain, even a French one? Jared was perishing to know, but he supposed he'd been cruel enough already.

He apologized once more in gentler tones, and Maria became composed enough to face him again.

"So," he said, patting her hand. "I believe it is the custom for a gentleman to offer his valentine some small gift, a token. What would you like? Anything but a fan," he added, eyeing the ivory sticks she wielded with distaste. "You're already armed to the teeth with those."

"I don't want anything from you," she began primly. Then she paused, a considering light coming into her eyes. A thoughtful frown marred her brow for a moment, then she said, "Perhaps you could do me one small favor."

"And what would that be?" he asked warily.

"How ungracious. You should have replied, 'Anything you desire, milady.'"

"I might have, but I remember all too well some of the crack-brained notions you used to have of what a gentleman should do to honor a lady."

"I'm not asking you to fight a duel or wrestle lions." She lowered her eyes in demure fashion. "It is only that you prevented me from delivering a valentine this morning. I was wondering if you might carry it for me now."

Jared folded his arms, issuing a snort of disbelief. "If that doesn't take the prize. Not only did the woman forget this is the tenth anniversary of our unwedding. Now she wants me to play Cupid in her romance with another man."

"The valentine is not for another man. It is a token of my friendship for a young lady, Miss Lucas."

It was unaccountable, the stab of relief he felt. But he demanded, "Why don't you walk over and hand Miss Lucas the valentine yourself?"

Maria plucked at the gilt embroidery threads on her gown. "That—that could prove a little awkward."

"Could it, indeed?"

"Yes, you see, she is the Duke of Sheffield's niece, and His Grace is a remarkably cruel guardian, not permitting that poor girl to have any friends."

"Especially not ones with a proclivity for meddling."

Color flamed high in Maria's cheeks. "I don't meddle."

"Not much, you don't. Even I have heard of your matchmaking activities. I daresay if there's ever another flood, you'll be called upon to captain the ark. But, Maria, I believe Miss Lucas is already paired off."

"Most unhappily so."

"Still, it is none of your affair, my girl. The chit is Sheffield's legal ward, and from what I've seen of her, a silly little ninnyhammer, not worth bothering your head over. You'd best leave Miss Lucas to sort out her own problems."

"What heroic advice," she snapped.

"It's practical advice. Sheffield has a curst vindictive temper when anyone annoys him. Once he had a fellow barred from membership in Boodle's simply because the poor clod had the ill luck to spill wine upon His Grace's sleeve."

"Happily, I am not planning to apply for membership at Boodle's."

"And then there was that young member of Parliament who outbid Sheffield on a horse he wanted. The duke made certain he lost his seat in Commons and was utterly ruined."

"I've never been interested in politics."

"I know that," Jared said with a touch of exasperation. Maria had always had her lovely head poked too far in some faerie-tale castle in the clouds. It would seem she still hadn't come down to the ground. No matter what he said to warn her about Sheffield, she was refusing to listen, her lips pursed into such a stubborn line, Jared had the urge to shake some sense into her.

He was marshaling further arguments when she disarmed him with a sudden winsome smile, a gentle pressure of her hand upon his.

"Jared, I'm not a complete widgeon. I know what a bully Sheffield can be, and I have no desire to provoke him. But his poor little niece is so isolated, so frightened of the prospect of being shipped off to marry some baronet she's never even met. I've simply been trying to offer her a bit of comfort, be a friend to her. Is that so terrible?"

"No, if that's as far as it goes."

"You've seen the valentine for yourself that I want to give her. What a harmless bit of nonsense it is. You even remarked yourself how dreadful the poetry was."

"Yes." He frowned. "It seems a deuced odd sentiment for one woman to send another."

"Miss Lucas and I are both fond of heroes 'bold and true.'" Maria leaned forward, making him aware of the sweet, heady scent of her perfume, the way tho candlelight caught the golden highlights of her hair, the intoxicating rise and fall of her breasts beneath the bodice of her gown.

"It would take no effort at all for you to slip Miss Lucas the valentine. Please, Jared."

It was a thoroughly feminine trick, the way her melting blue eyes pleaded with him through the thickness of her lashes. And it was little wonder that women used such a ploy. It worked wonderfully well.

Jared held out his hand. "Here. Give me the blasted thing."

Maria gave a glad cry. As she fished the sadly crumpled paper heart out of her reticule, she flashed him a dazzling smile.

As he studied the tempting line of those full, pouting lips, it occurred to him that he should have held out for a greater reward. But then again, he'd already gotten his ears soundly boxed once today.

He'd just accepted the valentine from Maria when he became aware of his uncle's approach. Lord Brixted was sweating from his exertions in the first dance with the woman who had ended up drawing him for her valentine, the dowager Lady Yarby, a hefty female who could likely have outridden, outdanced, and outwrestled every man in the room.

The earl stalked towards Jared and Maria, his chest puffed out. He reminded Jared of nothing so much as a bantam rooster spoiling for a fight.

Concealing his amusement, Jared rose to his feet and greeted his lordship with a solemn bow. "Well, Uncle! Did you enjoy your dance with Lady Yarby?"

"You infernal cur!" Lord Brixted muttered in Jared's ear.

"Alas, it would seem I have been demoted again," Jared murmured back.

His lordship quivered with all the rage he was unable to express. But he turned to Maria and managed a creditable leg. "Contessa, I trust you will favor me with the next dance. It is rather selfish of my nephew to keep you sitting here merely because he is unable to oblige you."

A shocked protest escaped Maria, but Jared intervened. The last thing he wanted from her was any hint of pity.

"I have no objections to Maria standing up with you, Uncle," Jared said with his most charming smile. "I am happy to lend you *my* valentine for the space of a dance."

This pointed reminder of how Jared had filched Maria away was enough to cause his lordship to choke. Jared feared his relative would have a fit of apoplexy before the night was over. But Lord Brixted ground his teeth and offered Maria his arm.

Yet as she glided away with the earl, Jared almost regretted having acquiesced so tamely. The next tune that the orchestra struck up was a waltz, and it seemed to Jared that his uncle's hand rested too intimately at Maria's waist, that he held her a bit too close.

Yet Maria didn't appear to mind. She looked up at Lord Brixted, smiling and talking as though enjoying herself. Jared had to grudgingly admit the old fellow didn't cut too bad a figure by candlelight. His stark black evening clothes became him far better than that ridiculous bottle green coat had done. With his hair smoothed back, his lordship even contrived to appear a mature gentleman of some distinction, with an astonishing amount of grace left in his step.

Amazing what a good corset could do for a man, Jared reflected cynically. But then perhaps he was just indulging in a bit of sour grapes because he had never been able to waltz with Maria. The dance had been unheard-of during the days of their courtship.

If the waltz had been popular then, maybe he wouldn't have found dancing with her such a chore. He could almost imagine what it would be like to feel her in his arms, the warmth of her hand in his as they twirled about the floor, the sparkling glow from the chandelier caught in her eyes.

Sighing, he rubbed the side of his injured leg, for the first time in a long time, knowing the bitterness of regret. But he was quick to shrug it off and set out to deliver the valentine as he had promised Maria.

It proved an easy enough errand. Sheffield himself was waltzing at the moment, and Miss Lucas had been left amid a cluster of clucking matrons. But Jared had ever been an expert at culling the female he wanted out of the herd. Just like a well-trained sheep dog, he thought with a grin.

He soon had Miss Lucas pulled to one side and was slipping the paper heart into her hands.

She turned bright pink and stammered, "Oh, sir, I—I—"

"Just tuck that beneath your shawl," he said

with a wink. "I believe it's something you've been expecting from a friend."

"But I had no idea it would be you—that you would be the one who— Oh!" She heaved a tremulous breath. "Thank you, Sir Jared. And don't worry. I remember the code."

"Code?" Jared echoed.

But Miss Lucas was already skittering away from him like a timid mouse. She only paused long enough to cast back a glance filled with adoration as though he were her long-awaited savior.

"Just a simple valentine. All fun and nonsense," Jared muttered under his breath. "Oh, Maria, you little wretch."

He glanced towards the dancers. Maria chanced to be twirling past at that moment, and she shot Jared a brilliant smile.

He shook his head. She'd once been one of the most transparent females he'd ever known. He wondered when she'd learned to be so devious.

Coded valentines! Jared wasn't often prey to premonitions, but he was having a devil of a one now. Delivering a paper heart to Miss Lucas. Such an innocent request, it had seemed. Why then did he have this strong feeling he'd just done something he was going to heartily regret?

Chapter 5

Maria seldom left any ball or party before midnight, and she was almost sorry she had done so tonight. Compared to the warmth and glitter of the earl's drawing room, a church graveyard was a cold and lonely place.

The wind whipped around the corner of the church, blowing snow across the headstones, pale and stark in the moonlight. The timeworn monuments stood bearing silent testimony to those whose joys, sorrows, and follies had long ago faded to dust, frozen and forgotten beneath the snow-shrouded mounds of earth.

Maria huddled deeper in her cloak and shivered, wondering where she'd ever gotten the notion that a graveyard on a cold winter night would be the perfect place for a secret rendezvous. True, it did have the advantage of being a quarter of a mile away from the manor, well out of range of the Duke of Sheffield's single piercing eye.

But Maria wondered if Miss Lucas would be able to figure out where the place was after she had deciphered Maria's instructions. And even if she did, would the girl then have the courage and resourcefulness to join Maria there at the appointed hour?

Maria was left with the discomfited feeling that she had not planned this out very carefully. But only time would tell.

Pacing up and down to keep warm, she hummed snatches of a waltz to keep her spirits up, and those beneath their graves firmly tamped down. Jared had always laughed at her superstitious belief in specters, and for the most part, she had outgrown such foolish notions.

Except in moonlit graveyards at the stroke of midnight. To keep more lurid imaginings at bay, Maria thought back instead to the Valentine's soiree. Most times she never left any ball until the crack of dawn, until her dancing slippers were nigh worn through. She waltzed, sipped champagne, flirted like a greedy child surfeiting herself on sweetmeats. Perhaps she was still attempting to capture those lost years of her girlhood when she had been permitted to attend no parties at all, when Papa had forced upon her an existence almost as reclusive as his own.

If Mama had but lived . . . But thoughts of her poor, unhappy mother were always melancholy, even more so in this mournful empty churchyard. Maria resolutely set those memories aside, puzzling out instead why she, who so adored balls, had not been having as good a time as usual tonight.

After she had stood up with the earl, she had been claimed by other partners and had danced every dance, as much to avoid Jared as anything else. She'd seen him deliver the valentine, but he'd looked far from pleased with her.

Perhaps he'd seen through her protestations of innocence, realized there was some plot afoot between herself and Miss Lucas. But it was none of Jared's concern, even if he had agreed to act as her go-between. He'd owed Maria that much. It was his fault she'd been unable to deliver the valentine herself in the first place.

So tossing her head, she'd ignored Jared's glower and spun through dance after dance, partner after partner. But somehow the exercise had proved less than satisfactory, though the musicians were most accomplished and so many of her partners had been handsome, charming.

But there had been only one man she truly wished to dance with, and dancing with that man was quite impossible. Maria picked up a stray branch and caught herself etching out Jared's name in the snow. She sighed. Damn him! It was difficult to admit, but he had succeeded in stirring to life old feelings she'd thought long dead.

But perhaps she was being too hard on herself. After all, she had once been thoroughly infatuated with the man. One could hardly be expected to forget one's first love entirely, even if one had been wise enough to outgrow it.

If only Jared hadn't consented to perform upon the pianoforte tonight. He'd always possessed a natural musical ability, but he could rarely be induced to play. He'd only done so for her when they were courting because he had been appalled by Maria's ignorance. Like so much else of her education, music, too, had been neglected. She could plunk out a few sentimental ballads by ear and that was all.

It had been Jared who had introduced her to the fire, the passion, the grandeur, of the great composers, Brahms, Beethoven, Mozart. Yet strangely tonight, it had been he who had elected to entertain the company with one of those old ballads he had always despised.

He'd played as well as ever, but his voice, that magnificent baritone, had somehow grown richer and stronger than she even remembered. Those haunting notes had seemed to go right through her, settle deep in her heart. Perhaps it had all been a trick of the candlelight, but the cynical lines of Jared's face appeared to soften as he had crooned about love lost, things that might have been, things that could never be.

He bore about him the look of misplaced innocence, a tarnished knight forever barred from seeking the Holy Grail. Watching him, listening to him, Maria had had to fight off the urge to weep.

Such a promising young man, Jared had been, possessed of so many talents, a bruising rider and athlete, a brilliant scholar, clever with both pen and in conversation, a gifted musician. All talents that he appeared to have just thrown away.

It grieved her. The gossip she heard about how Jared spent his days—drinking, gaming, chasing lightskirts, always one step away from debtors' prison or an early grave. What had happened to him? Had he become so embittered over his wartime injury or was he simply one of those men who never seemed to find a sense of purpose?

Maria could not believe his behavior had anything to do with a certain cold February day when he had waited in vain for her to arrive at church. No, the end of their foolish romance had been farce, not tragedy, and Jared had been the first to recover. Not a fortnight later, Maria had seen him out with Cecilia

King, teaching that bold piece to drive his curricle, kissing her.

Maria pursed her lips at the memory, but she supposed she couldn't fault Jared for what he had done with his life. She was not certain she'd made such a sterling use of her own.

She might well be a wealthy woman, independent, but she was also rapidly approaching thirty, childless, husbandless, and without any close family ties. She'd hoped she'd at least done some good, helping others. She'd never been able to make a faerie tale of her own existence, but she'd done her best to spin them for everyone else she met.

She'd matched up many lovelorn women, from the daughters of lords even to some of her own maidservants. They'd all ridden blissfully off into the sunset with the prince of their dreams, be he a baronet or just a simple footman. Maria often wondered. After she'd succeeded in pairing off everyone she knew, would she wake up someday and find herself an old woman, left quite alone, her only future a fading tombstone like those that surrounded her now?

It was a grim and depressing reflection, especially when she realized an open grave yawned not two yards from where she paced. At least, it was half an open grave. The frozen earth appeared to have presented a difficulty, and the grave remained rather shallow.

Water had filled the hole and frozen over, rendering it even more dark and uninviting. Peering into it, Maria shuddered. She was trembling even before two strong hands seized her from behind, hauling her back from the grave.

She let out a piercing shriek and wrenched about like a wild thing, flailing out against the tall, cloaked specter that loomed up before her. But her fist struck up against flesh and bone. Unless ghosts had taken to wearing curly-brimmed beavers, it was no phantom who had seized her, but a man.

He staggered back, one hand clutched to his face, a familiar voice growling, "Ow! Damn it, woman! That's the second time today you've pounded me."

"J Jarod?" Her heart still thudding from her fright, Maria peered into the darkness.

Jared stepped out of the shadows cast by the church, moonlight illuminating his disgruntled countenance. "Ill met by moonlight, proud Titania."

Maria heaved a tremulous breath, part relief, part indignation. "What are you doing here?"

"Quoting Shakespeare. Having my nose broken. Is it bleeding?"

"No, but it would serve you right if it was, creeping up on me that way."

"I was trying to keep you from tumbling into that hole."

"It's a dangerous practice disturbing faeries at their nighttime revels. Just like what happened to Bottom, I might decide to turn you into an ass."

"I think you've done a fair job of that already," he said acidly. "So you left the ball early because you had a headache? Is there some new cure for the megrims to be found in graveyards or would this little midnight jaunt have something to do with that harmless little valentine I passed to Miss Lucas?"

"You read my valentine. You figured out the

code!" Maria cried with a stomp of her foot. "That's how you knew where to find me."

"Give me a little credit, madam. A babe could have guessed you were up to some mischief and trailed you down from the house."

"Then you can just trail yourself right away from here again."

But Jared moved towards her, his face so dark with menace Maria almost thought she might have preferred it to have been a ghost that had frightened her instead. He seized her roughly by the shoulders.

"I'm not going anywhere until you tell me what devilment you've gotten me involved in."

"You! You are not involved."

"Then maybe you ought to make that clear to Miss Lucas. When I gave her that ridiculous valentine, I think the empty-headed chit believed it was from me. She spent the rest of the evening gazing at me as though I were her conquering hero."

"She believed that? Blast it all, Jared. I asked you to do me one small favor and you made a wretched tangle of—"

But Maria checked herself. It likely wasn't prudent, voicing complaints to a man who was already looking as though he wanted to strangle her.

She forced a conciliatory smile to her lips. "That is, I am most grateful to you, Jared, for delivering the valentine. But why didn't you make it clear to Miss Lucas that you were only my messenger?"

"Why didn't you make it clear I was delivering secrets?"

"Because you wouldn't have been so obliging. You would have treated me to some sarcastic lecture or—or—" She wriggled away from beneath his grasp. "What odds does it make now? It's done. You delivered the valentine. I'm sorry I tricked you, but I was waxing desperate. I had to get that message to Miss Lucas."

"Why? What is so cursed urgent, Maria?"

She bit down upon her lip and considered concocting some fantastic tale. But beneath Jared's hard gaze, her gift for fiction deserted her.

"Very well," she said. "You might as well know the truth. I am trying to help Miss Lucas escape from her guardian."

Jared swore. "I was afraid you harbored some fool notion like that. Damnation, Maria! Have you never considered the legalities? The duke could have you brought up on charges if you make off with his ward."

"I might have known that would be your attitude," Maria sniffed. "That is why I chose not to tell you anything."

"It would be the attitude of any sane person, of any magistrate you might eventually have to face."

"I don't care. Sheffield is a monster, forcing that poor child to marry some old hermit of a baronet."

"All the girl has to do is say no. These aren't medieval times. A woman can't be forced into marriage without her consent."

"You know a sweet, gentle girl like Miss Lucas would not have the courage to stand up to Sheffield."

"Then what makes you think she would have the fortitude to meet you in a graveyard at the dead of night?"

"Because—because—" Maria threw her hands

wide in exasperation. That had always been the frustrating thing about arguing with Branden. When all else failed, he resorted to logic. A most unfair tactic in Maria's opinion, because when had the human heart ever had a thing to do with logic?

"Miss Lucas will come because she's desperate," Maria concluded. "Because sometimes it's easier to run away from your misery than to face it."

And she ought to know, Maria thought bitterly. She'd done the same thing herself, many years ago, fleeing her father's tyranny and the sight of Jared giving Miss King driving lessons. Of course, Maria had been fortunate. She had had an elderly aunt to help her. Poor Miss Lucas had no one.

That thought helped strengthen Maria in her resolve, and she needed that brace as Jared continued, "One would have to be desperate to seek out a cemetery at night. All these corpses but a few shovels full of dirt beneath our feet, all those moldering bones. The wind howling, sounding like tormented souls, unquiet spirits. Br-r-r." Jared gave a mock shudder.

That same shudder seemed to echo through her own frame. But Maria set her jaw stubbornly. She knew exactly what he was trying to do, frighten her into leaving, giving up her rendezvous with Miss Lucas.

"It is far too cold," she retorted. "I doubt even ghosts would care to walk abroad tonight."

"I shouldn't worry so much about ghosts as grave robbers."

"Grave robbers?"

"Yes, I hear it's become quite a profitable business, digging up fresh corpses, selling them off to medical students for dissection."

Maria stole an uneasy glance around her, half expecting to see some ghoulish creatures, more goblinlike than human, come slinking from behind the line of trees, armed with their shovels, their decaying teeth glinting in the moonlight. Sometimes it was a curse to be afflicted with such a vivid imagination.

But she said stoutly, "Actually I am in sympathy with those poor medical students. They shouldn't have to steal bodies when they are only trying to benefit mankind with their research."

"I would never want anyone sawing away at my corpse."

"Then you are quite selfish, Branden. I'm sure I would be happy to offer up my body if it would do you any good."

Jared's voice dropped, whiskey-warm. "Now, that is quite the most sensible suggestion you've made all evening."

"Oh, you! You know what I meant!" Her cheeks flaming, Maria tugged the hood of her cloak up over her bonnet, retreating deeper into the sheltering folds. "I don't know why you should have come here plaguing me, but I wish you would go away again. It surely cannot concern you what risks I am taking. No one is asking *you* to play the hero."

She thought he flinched a little at that, but he replied in his usual drawling tone, "One would be an idiot if one did. But then your Miss Lucas is something of a fool. I just want it made plain to the chit that I have nothing to do with this escapade."

"Never fear," Maria said. "I'll make certain she understands that nothing is to be expected of Sir Jared Branden."

"Good. Then I'll leave you to your midnight vigil, Titania."

"Do so at once, sir." She swept around regally, presenting him with the line of her back.

"Good night, milady." His voice mocked her. She heard the crunch of his boots retreating upon the frozen snow. But there was a pause as he called back, "Oh, and, Contessa, if any corpse snatchers do turn up, be sure and point out to them that grave in the corner. It looks the freshest."

Maria quivered with anger. But by the time she thought of a crushing enough retort and turned around to deliver it, Jared was gone, vanishing as suddenly as he had appeared.

The silent churchyard appeared more lonely and empty than ever. Her shoulders sagged a little. She could scarce believe that he'd really done it, just gone off and left her.

But what had she expected? That he would stay and offer to help her save Miss Lucas? Disinterested knight errantry had never been Jared's style, and the years only appeared to have rendered him more cynical.

She hated to acknowledge the fact, but she might have welcomed his support, the comfort of his strong, powerful presence on a cold, dark night like this. Plotting the rescue of Miss Lucas was the most difficult and possibly dangerous thing Maria had ever attempted. But Jared would have been clever enough to—

No. Maria checked the idea, furious at herself for

even thinking it. That seemed too much as though she required Jared's services, and she didn't need him, not for anything. She'd been capable for some time now of handling anything that came along, distressed, lovelorn young ladies, villainous dukes, or even . . . grave robbers.

Maria swallowed, eyeing the shadows cast by headstones. She tried not to think about rotting corpses or the men who handled them, their talonlike fingernails encrusted with dirt from the graves. She had just convinced herself that Jared's taunting remarks had not frightened her in the least when the stillness of night was broken by the sharp crack of a twig.

Maria tensed, listening. It might have been easier to hear without her pulse thundering in her ears. But the next sound came louder, more clearly. Surely that had been a footfall. Spinning around, Maria peered towards the line of oak trees that marked the outer limits of the cemetery. It was not just her imagination. She was certain she saw a shadowy form lurking behind the trunk of the broadest tree.

"Miss Lucas?" she called hopefully.

No reply. Would the foolish child really linger there, too timid to come forward, terrifying Maria by her silence? Maybe it was not Miss Lucas at all, but Branden come creeping back. It would be just like him to spring at her again, play some hellacious prank to frighten her out of her wits. Wouldn't it be? she thought weakly.

If Jared was plotting such a thing, the next headstone in this graveyard was going to be his own.

Stepping forward, Maria ignored the thud of her

heart. "Miss Lucas? Branden?" she called in as firm a voice as she could muster. "Whoever is hiding there, come out at once."

A cloaked figure melted out of the shadows. Moonshine reflected his gaunt form in a dagger of light. Maria's heart leapt into her throat.

Sheffield.

She could not have been more appalled than a damsel who had gone poking in a forbidden cave, only to arouse a sleeping dragon. And at the moment, His Grace looked very dragonlike, a cloud of frosty air issuing from his pinched nostrils, his single cold eye fixing Maria with an icy stare.

He stalked forward, his cloak billowing behind him, clutching a silver-tipped walking stick like the devil's own scepter. His lips thinned in a smile that mingled triumph with malevolence, and Maria knew in that instant that all was discovered, the plot unraveled.

But she contrived to meet the duke with a bold front. "Your—Your Grace. What a surprise."

"Is it, my dear contessa?" he purred. "Did you think you were the only one interested in graveyards?

"I believe this belongs to you." Sheffield brandished the tattered valentine she had sent to Miss Lucas.

"For me?" Maria said. "Why, Your Grace, I had no idea you cared. Alas, I fear I'm already spoken for this Valentine's Day."

His thin smile fading, Sheffield slowly crushed the paper heart in his leather glove. Then he let it fall from his hand, the wind catching the mangled valentine, tumbling it past the headstones.

"I am in no humor for these games, madam."

He took another step closer. Now only the narrow width of a grave separated them. Light and shadow played across the silver-gray of his wig and black eye patch, a face more ravaged by a bent for cruelty than any disease.

Maria fought down a strong urge to flee. He's naught but a bully, she reminded herself over and over again, reveling in the fear and misery he inflicts upon others. How often had she had occasion to repeat the same litany about her own father.

"It was you who had that valentine delivered to my niece," Sheffield said coldly.

Maria raised her chin in defiance. "And what if I did? Is that now accorded a crime? I believe even prisoners at Newgate are permitted to receive visitors and messages."

"Not when those messages deal with plots to escape."

"I—I don't know what you are talking about."

"It seems that, like you, my ward was also afflicted with a headache and left the ball early. I went up to her room to check upon her and found both the valentine and the message she had deciphered, the one commanding her to meet you here. She'd just left it lying about on the sitting room table. Selina is not a very bright girl."

Maria grimaced, suppressing the urge to agree with him. How could the foolish child have been so careless? But perhaps the carelessness had been more Maria's. She should have found a better way to communicate with Miss Lucas, arranged a more reasonable meeting time and place. Maria was left with a sickened sense that instead of helping Miss

93

Lucas, she'd only made matters that much worse for the young woman.

Maria moistened her lips, feeling almost ill with dread. "What—What did you do to Miss Lucas when you discovered the valentine?"

"Nothing."

Maria had started to breathe a sigh of relief, but she checked it as Sheffield continued, "Nothing . . . *yet*. I will deal with Selina all in good time. At the moment, I am more vexed with your part in this. You have no right, madam, encouraging my niece to defy me."

"And you have no right forcing her into a marriage she doesn't want."

"She is my ward. I shall do what I like with her, and as for you, Contessa . . ." He tapped his cane against his gloved hand in menacing fashion. "Be warned. I have heard of your penchant for meddling in the affairs of others. Lesser men may tolerate such impertinence, but I do not. I am not a man who would enjoy being made to play the fool."

"Why not?" Maria snapped. "You do it so well."

Something flared in Sheffield's eye and she saw at once she'd goaded him too far. He closed the distance between them, his hand closing about her wrist.

"Let me go," she said, her pulse quickening with a mixture of fear and anger as she struggled to be free.

But his grip only tightened cruelly. "Nay, Contessa. I have no tolerance for bold women with sharp tongues. I meant to let you off lightly this time, but it is clear you are badly in need of a man to teach you a lesson."

He twisted her about and raised his cane, preparing to bring it crashing down upon her backside. But before she could react to defend herself, something happened that startled her as much as Sheffield.

The duke flinched, reeling from a hard-packed ball of snow that exploded against the side of his face. He released Maria as several more icy missiles found their mark, the last one sending a cascade of snow down the collar of Sheffield's cloak.

Maria stood gaping as a shiver coursed through Sheffield, his face twisting into an expression somewhere between astonishment and outrage. She had a feeling it was the first time anyone had ever dared pelt His Grace of Sheffield with a snowball. And somehow it did not surprise her to see who had been so bold.

Once again materializing like a phantom out of the night, Jared came tearing across the churchyard, only slightly hampered by his awkward gait. He seized Maria about the waist, dragging her to his side.

She did not know what had brought Jared back, but she could have sagged against him, trembling with relief. Except that Sheffield had recovered from his initial shock.

Wiping the snow from his face, the duke sputtered, "Branden! You—You buffoon!"

"Careful," Jared admonished, lightly tossing up and catching the snowball he still carried in his right hand. "It's not wise to insult a man who still possesses ammunition."

Sheffield went white with a rage as icy as the snow. He tugged at the cane, sliding a hidden sword stick from its sheath, the blade gleaming lethally in the moonlight.

A horrified cry breached Maria's lips, but Jared only drawled, "Damn. A man who takes his snowfights seriously."

Was Jared mad, taunting Sheffield that way? The duke stalked forward, his hand trembling with barely contained fury, as he leveled the tip of his sword at Jared's chest.

Jared attempted to thrust Maria behind him, but she resisted, crying, "Stop it. Both of you. Your Grace, you can hardly fight a duel over something as foolish as a snowball."

"Correct me if I'm wrong, my dear," Jared said. "But I think both men have to be armed for it to be called a duel."

Maria glared up at him. The man was but a breath away from having a blade thrust through his heart and he was doing naught but making jests. Maria feared she would be obliged to tackle Sheffield herself as Jared threw up his hands in mocking surrender, still holding that ridiculous clump of snow.

"Skewer me, if you feel you must, Your Grace," he invited amicably. "What a page that will make in the history of the noble family of Sheffield. I can hear it being bruited about at White's even now. The Honorable Affair of the Snowball."

Maria stifled a groan. Jared was a dead man. But to her astonishment, Branden's teasing words seemed to give His Grace pause. After another tense moment, the duke lowered his sword and drew in a deep, cleansing breath. He slowly resheathed the blade back into the cane.

Maria did not know what she wanted to do more, sob with relief or pummel Jared with her fists. Of the three of them, only Jared appeared unperturbed as His Grace rasped, "You disappoint me, Branden. I'd hoped you had more sense than this."

"Ah well, that seems to be my lot in life. Always crushing someone's good opinion of me."

The duke's lips thinned. "You will regret it if you allow the contessa to draw you into her meddling ways. But I suppose there are some men who cannot resist allowing a woman to make a fool of them."

"Yes," Jared sighed. "And why must I always be one of them?"

Maria stepped indignantly away from him. "Sir Jared has nothing to do with me or my plans, Your Grace," she said. "His being here tonight was pure chance and—"

"Spare me any more of your pretty lies, milady," the duke cut her off. "It is obvious to me that Branden is your lover and is as neck-deep in this plot as you are. He would be better advised to keep you in bed, where you belong."

Maria gasped, but His Grace continued, "From here on, let both of you be warned. Stay away from my niece or suffer the consequences."

With an arrogant swirl of his cloak, His Grace pivoted on his heel and stalked off into the night. Speechless with outrage, Maria watched his retreat, then turned to Jared, seething with her indignation.

"Will you just permit that vile man to get away with that? Insulting me? Threatening us?"

"What would you have me do?" Jared asked,

dropping the remains of his snowball, dusting the fine white powder from his gloves. "It would appear my weapon has crumbled apart."

He spoke with an air of laconic detachment that Maria found infuriating. "You might have done something a shade more heroic than hurl snowballs."

"In case you've forgotten, the duke had a sword, and I have none. I fear I don't run any better these days than I dance. Of course, I'm always delighted to impale myself in your honor, Contessa, but I can't see what use I would be to you dead."

That was Jared. Always mocking, always practical. Maria feared she was being unreasonable. She didn't know what more she expected of him. Perhaps at least some fierce threat of what Jared would do if Sheffield menaced her again, some tender expression of concern at what Maria had suffered at the duke's hands.

She heaved a deep sigh. "Do you really think His Grace is capable of murder?"

"Probably not. It would be far too awkward, all that much blood, two bodies to be disposed of in a frozen churchyard. Very inconvenient. And just like me, I've a notion His Grace doesn't appreciate being inconvenienced."

Maria rebelliously scuffed the toe of her boot, dislodging some snow from the side of a tombstone. "Then why didn't you tell His Grace plainly that you were not involved? You let him walk away thinking that we are lovers. And if it comes to that, why did you even come back here at all?"

Jared shrugged. "I was strolling back to the manor, admiring the stars, when I saw His Grace heading in your direction. He did not appear in a particularly pleasant mood, and I guess I kept remembering your charming offer that I could have your body. I preferred to collect it while it was still warm."

Their eyes met. Maria tried to cling to her sense of angry hurt and resentment, but she found she could not hold out against the teasing humor she found in his gaze, the tender light of amusement. Maria hardly realized she was trembling with reaction from her recent fright until Jared stepped forward and wrapped his arms about her.

She stiffened, resisting for a moment, but the strong curve of his shoulder proved far too tempting. She buried her face against his cloak, the fabric rough beneath her cheek, redolent with his strong, masculine scent.

"Oh, Jared," she said. "I quite detest myself. I fear I've made a botch of everything and I allowed that beastly man to intimidate me."

"You were a lion," he murmured, resting his head against the top of her hood. "Sheffield can thank his lucky stars I arrived to rescue him when I did, before you showed him your punishing right."

A reluctant chuckle escaped Maria. Jared cupped his fingers beneath her chin, tipping her face up towards his. An expression of rare seriousness darkened his eyes.

"Maria, you must heed me this time. I've always thought Sheffield was a little queer in the attic, and his sanity appears to be dangling by an even looser thread these days. You'd best stay clear of him."

"But am I just to forget about poor Miss Lucas?" she protested.

"Your Miss Lucas is a pretty peagoose. Such addlepated women always seem to do all right for themselves in the end."

"You wouldn't say that if you had seen Miss Lucas the first night I met her. It was at a Christmas party. All the other young people were laughing, stealing kisses under the mistletoe, while she, poor child, was huddled in the window seat, trying to stifle her sobs. It was enough to have melted your heart."

"But I don't have one, remember? You told me so a long time ago when you were busy breaking it."

His eyes clouded, and for a moment Maria almost thought he was in earnest. Then his mouth quirked into his usual mocking smile.

Lowering her eyes, she said, "Please don't make jests, Jared. It is hardly necessary to reminisce about all the foolish things we once said to each other."

"I agree. We both had a tendency to talk too much. We still do."

And leaning forward, he silenced her with a swift kiss. So sudden, so unexpected, Maria was at first too startled to respond. The feel of his mouth on hers was warm, rough, sweet. As he gathered her in his arms, she felt the familiar thrill course through her that Jared's kisses had always been able to induce.

But she drew back, protesting, "No, Jared. You— You mustn't."

"That's what you were forever telling me. But where's the harm in one little kiss?" he coaxed. "If not for old times' sake, then because you are my valentine."

"But Valentine's Day is over, sir."

"You don't understand the custom. You are to be mine for the rest of the year."

"Oh! I suppose one can hardly argue with custom," she said rather breathlessly as Jared drew her closer. One could hardly argue with anything as his lips claimed hers. Feelings she'd sought to deny sprang to life again, like flames banked on a hearth encountering dried kindling.

Hot, passionate, seeking, his embrace was as she'd remembered, and yet . . . there was a tenderness to Jared's kiss that had never existed before, that not only stirred her blood, but branded itself into her heart as well. Wrapping her arms about his neck, she melted against him, returning his kiss, tenderness for tenderness, fire for fire.

When he released her, they gazed into each other's eyes and it was as though a veil had parted between them, leaving them both feeling a little vulnerable, exposed.

For once, Jared was not so quick at finding something to say.

"Maria, I . . ." he began tentatively. "It—It might go better between us this time."

"It might," she agreed softly. "We are older, wiser."

"I don't know about the wiser part, but certainly older."

After another heartbeat of hesitation, Maria suggested almost shyly, "I've rented a house for the Season in town. You could call upon me. We—We could take tea."

"I am devilishly fond of tea," he said huskily, breathing kisses against her temple, her eyelids, the curve of her cheek.

Maria shivered at the delightful sensations he aroused. "And—And we could have ... conversations."

"I adore conversation." His lips teased the corner of her mouth in a way that was tantalizing, sensual.

Maria heaved a long, blissful sigh. "And we might even still find a way to save Miss Lucas."

Jared stiffened, his mouth but a breath away from her own. Maria's lips parted in invitation, but it was one he did not accept. He drew back, blinking like a man who had suddenly been rudely slapped awake.

Abruptly he set her away from him, that familiar cynical look she so hated creeping back into his eyes. He slowly shook his head.

"Tell me something, Maria. Just where did you learn these little tricks? From your Count Machiavelli?"

"Tricks?" Maria echoed, stunned herself by the abrupt change in him. "I'm afraid I don't know what you mean."

"These new skills of seduction, the melting look with the eyes, the breathy voice, the soft, pouting lips. All ploys to twist a man round your finger so that he will do any damfool thing you suggest."

"Seduction!" she gasped. The heat of passion that had warmed her cheeks became fire of a different sort. "It was you who wanted to kiss me."

"A desire that you were quick to turn to your own advantage," he said. "If you expect me to risk my neck over that Lucas chit for a few of your favors, you'd best forget it. Unless you're prepared to offer me a great deal more than kisses."

"How dare you!" Maria trembled with a mixture of raw hurt and outrage. "How dare you imply that I would— Oh! You're worse than a barbarian. Worse than the devil himself. Worse than—than *Sheffield*."

"Now you've utterly wounded me, Contessa."

Maria's eyes glittered with furious tears. "And to think for one moment I'd almost imagined that things had changed, that things might possibly be different between us."

She choked back the lump in her throat and paced off a few steps until she was able to face him with a modicum of dignity. "No, Sir Jared, I am not offering you anything for aiding Miss Lucas. Rescuing a lady in distress is something a man with any nobility would do without expecting a bribe."

"Only the crack-brained heroes in those books you used to read."

"They weren't crack-brained. They were the embodiments of the ideal, Lancelot, Galahad, Don Quixote."

"Don Quixote?" Jared had been looking grim, but he let out a whoop of laughter that only added fuel to Maria's ire. "That Spanish fellow who went around fighting windmills? Oh, very noble, that, Maria. So what if it made some poor farmer hopping mad?"

"It was the spirit of Don Quixote I'm talking about," she said through clenched teeth. "The spirit of chivalry, but you would know nothing about that and . . . and . . ." She trailed off into incoherency as

Jared continued to shake with laughter. "What is the use of even trying to talk to you?"

"There is none, I'm afraid," he said, rubbing at his eyes, composing himself. "At least, not until you are prepared to give up trying to make a hero of me." He swept her a mocking bow. "If you ever come to your senses someday, and feel the need of an ordinary man, you know where to find me."

"I don't need any man, ordinary or otherwise." With a proud toss of her head, she stalked past him, commencing the long, cold walk back to the manor.

She was aware of Jared keeping pace beside her, but she chose to ignore him. Those fleeting moments they had shared, those tender romantic kisses, now seemed but an illusion, the product of her imagination.

They spoke not a word to each other, not even when they arrived back at the house. They slipped in the side entrance that Maria had left unlocked. Branden, churl that he was, did not even trouble himself to hold the door for her.

He started up the servants' stair ahead of her, and Maria trailed after him, still seething. On the landing above, she could see her maid, a candle illuminating Alice's worried features.

Likely the woman had been pacing and fretting over Maria's safe return. But Maria did not rush ahead to reassure her. She could not permit Branden to escape without some efforts at having the final word.

Catching him by the sleeve, she forced him to halt midway up the stairs.

"Just let me tell you one more thing, sir," she

said fiercely. "No matter what you believe, heroes don't exist just in books."

"That's right. I keep forgetting. You were married to one once. The noble Count Macaroni."

The mention of the count made her wince, but she said, "My Roberto was a hero. You can rest assured he would have ridden to Miss Lucas's aide."

"But he was also stupid enough to fall off an Alp."

"It was not stupid. He was doing something noble even then." Maria faltered for a second before continuing. "There—There was a poor little lamb that had been caught in a rockslide. Its leg was broken, and Roberto was trying to rescue it."

"He sacrificed himself for a haunch of mutton? How utterly romantic." Jared launched into some long Italian quote. Maria did not understand enough of the language to comprehend, but from his unholy grin, she was certain he was saying something thoroughly abominable.

Maria was about to respond when she was distracted by an ungodly shriek from Alice. Maria glanced up, astonished to see her maid come hurtling down the stairs at Jared.

"What the devil—" Jared started to growl, but was cut off as Alice dealt him a sound box to the ears that sent him staggering back.

He stumbled down a few steps, cracking his head against an iron wall sconce. Clutching his brow, he reeled and would have fallen farther except that Maria seized his arm to steady him.

Her anger momentarily forgotten, Maria gasped, "Jared, are you all right?"

With a muffled oath, he shook her off. Taking his

hand away, he stared disgruntled at the blood staining his palm from a tiny cut on his temple. Then he gazed wrathfully at the trembling Alice. "What the blazes is the matter with you, woman?"

"Oh, take care, milady," Alice quavered, crouching against the wall. "The blow didn't work. He's going off into one of his fits again."

The murderous glare Jared shot at Alice was certainly enough to make the poor woman think so.

Maria interposed herself between them. "Don't be angry at Alice, Jared. I fear this was my doing. I told her you were mad."

"So I am! For ever having anything to do with you, madam." Shoving past her and the shrinking maid, Jared limped the rest of the way up the steps.

"But, Jared, please," Maria called, experiencing an unwelcome bite of remorse. "You need looking after, at least some sticking plaster for that cut."

"My valet will see to it. I intend to roust Frontenac to pack at once."

"Pack? Where are you going at this hour of the night?"

Jared paused on the landing to declare savagely, "Back to London. To someplace like White's where I'll be safe. Someplace where no women are allowed!"

And a few seconds later, Maria heard his bedchamber door shut with a slam that was loud enough to bring down the rafters.

Chapter 6

That blasted charley had seemed to lurk beneath the window of Jared's lodgings all night, bawling out that all was well. If he'd had a pistol, he would have shot the damned fellow, Jared reflected as he dragged himself out of bed to face the light of noon.

He'd always enjoyed the bustle of town life, but in the fortnight since he'd returned to London, every creaking carriage wheel, every street vendor's cry, every clatter of horses' hooves, only added to Jared's dark mood of irritation.

Staggering to the window, he wrenched the curtains closed, his head throbbing from more than just last night's excesses. Rummaging through the top bureau drawer, he cast linen stocks and sundry other articles of clothing aside, until he located a handkerchief.

He blew his nose gustily, and then gasped for breath as he was seized by a coughing spell. The violent hacking lasted for several moments and left him feeling rather weak. With a silent curse, he sagged down in a chair.

He'd caught a chill, most likely on the night that he'd gone chasing Maria on her moonlight revels.

And it served him right, too, damn fool that he'd been.

He should have known better than to get caught up in Titania's spell once more, to hang about a frozen churchyard trying to keep her out of mischief, protecting her from the consequences of her own folly. A protection for which the lady had shown precious little gratitude.

She'd wanted more from him. She'd wanted him to make a cake out of himself playing Don Quixote for that hen-witted Lucas chit, and she'd been willing to use every feminine charm she possessed. Melting in his arms, kissing him that way, making him believe for one absurd second there was a chance that she still . . .

No, that thought *was* absurd. Jared massaged his aching temples as though he would expunge the notion from his mind. Cynic that he was, he should have realized. He knew how women were, employing all their little wiles to get what they wanted from a man.

But that was the devil of it. Maria had always been different. His flaxen-haired maiden had been an innocent, totally without guile, devastating him with the honesty of her clear blue eyes.

But it appeared she had changed, and it was annoying. It was more than annoying, he thought with a weary sigh. It hurt like hell to think that she could pretend with him that way, hurt even more to realize that she still found him wanting, lacking in all the qualities she had ever desired in a man.

Qualities that she had apparently found in her precious Roberto, the great martyr of the Italian

Alps. But no, it had been the French ones, Jared corrected himself bitterly, then felt disgusted with the acid he felt churn through him.

He couldn't possibly be jealous of some ass of an Italian count, any more than he really cared what had happened with Maria in that churchyard. It was much easier to believe this ache that lodged in his chest was only the result of congestion.

He'd done his best to relieve it these past two weeks, taking the air every night at gaming hells, taverns, every sporting event that London offered this time of year. He'd ladled enough whiskey down his throat to have cured or killed an average man. Nothing seemed to help.

Ah, well, Jared thought with a philosophical shrug of his shoulders. He should have expected something like this. St. Valentine's never had been precisely his day.

His chest burned with another coughing fit as his valet entered the bedchamber. Frontenac leveled a deep frown at his master.

"Monsieur!" he exclaimed. "You should be in bed."

Anticipating the quip that rose to Jared's lips, the valet added dourly, "Alone."

"Strange," Jared drawled, "that's the same thing that doxy told me a few nights ago."

Frontenac turned bright red as he always did at any mention of amorous exploits, which was only added inducement for Jared to continue. He mimicked in a high falsetto, " 'La, sir, for all the interest you're showing, I might as well not even be here.'

'But I don't know what she was so indignant

about." Jared reverted to his normal tones. "She'd been well paid. If anybody should have been disappointed by my lack of performance, it should have been me."

"Uh, I believe these things happen to all gentlemen on occasion," Frontenac said uncomfortably. "Monsieur should not allow it to distress him."

"Oh, I wasn't distressed." Jared paused to sneeze into his handkerchief. "In fact, I'm having difficulty giving a damn about much of anything these days. I've even been lax in tormenting you, old fellow. I suppose it's the consequence of a stopped-up head."

"Or a stopped-up heart," Frontenac muttered.

"What?"

"*Rien*, monsieur." The valet moved briskly about, picking up the clothes Jared had littered across the room in his search for a handkerchief.

Jared had a feeling the valet had uttered some impertinence, but since that was nothing new and Jared felt a sudden chill course through him, he huddled closer to the fire and ignored Frontenac. The valet handed him the latest edition of the *Post*, and Jared opened it to the front page.

Even his eyes seemed aching and blurry this morning, and he had difficulty concentrating on the words. He became aware of Frontenac hovering at his elbow.

"Perhaps monsieur would wish me to send for the doctor?"

"Why? If you want me dead that much, my dear Frontenac, just dash my brains out with the poker and be done with it."

"It is not a matter of jest. Monsieur is very ill, and if I may say so—"

"You may not."

"Monsieur has done little to improve his condition by staying out each night until dawn."

"Have I been keeping you from your sleep, Frontenac? I told you, you needn't wait up for me. You solicitude about my health is touching, but I would prefer to have my breakfast."

"*Certainement,* monsieur. I thought a little thin gruel?"

"Only if you wish to wear it."

"And, monsieur, there is a most importunate gentleman waiting in the sitting room to have a word with you."

"How good of you to rush right in and inform me of that fact." With a sigh, Jared gave over his efforts to read the paper, and folded it up. "I suppose it's some wretched tradesman come to dun me for an unpaid account."

Frontenac looked deeply offended. "Would I permit a bill collector to descend upon monsieur before breakfast? *Non,* this person is a far more unsavory individual."

"Ah, one of my friends then."

"I trust not, monsieur." Frontenac sniffed. "But I believe monsieur has had dealings with the gentleman before. It is a Mr. Beamus."

"Beamus," Jared growled at his valet, annoyed with him for taking so long about imparting this information. He shoved to his feet. For several seconds his head reeled and he had to fight off another coughing spasm. The prospect of sagging back onto his bed had never been more inviting, but he ordered Frontenac to inform Beamus he would be out directly.

Some quarter of an hour later, Jared, clad in breeches and shirt, shrugged into a dressing gown. He was clean-shaven, at least enough for a meeting with Alfred Beamus, late of the Bow Street runners, thief taker extraordinaire.

Jared found the wiry little man warming his hands at the sitting room fire. Garbed in a dark, shabby coat, a modest low-crowned hat pulled low over his nondescript features, Beamus was the sort of man who could have blended in any street crowd, lost himself in any shadowed doorway.

At Jared's entrance into the room, Beamus came about, whipping off his hat and chirruping, "Good day, Sir Jared."

Jared stifled a cough behind his hand and motioned Beamus to a chair. As the man sat down with a flourish of his coattails, Beamus clucked his tongue and said, "Nasty cough, that, sir. Not feeling quite the thing this morning, are we?"

"I don't know about you, but I am fine," Jared snapped, beginning to feel irritated with all this discussion of his health. "You have a report to make to me, Mr. Beamus?"

"Aye, sir, such as it is." Beamus shrugged. "This is the queerest fetch I've ever been on, doing nothing but trailing after the lady in question, reporting her movements. I almost feel ashamed to be taking your money for such an easy task."

"Try to overcome your blushes," Jared said dryly. Beamus was a discreet man, ever speaking only of the "lady in question," the contessa's name never mentioned between them. But if anyone should be ashamed for having set a spy upon Maria, Jared reckoned it should be him. She would be furious if she ever found out, and Jared would be hard-pressed to explain his motives. He didn't fully comprehend them himself.

Perhaps it was the fact that his luck had turned lately and he'd been winning so much at the card tables. He was at a loss to know how to spend it. Odd how that happened when one was at one's most reckless and uncaring.

Besides, whether she liked it or not, Maria was his valentine. Jared owed her some token little present. The lady had gloves and fans aplenty, so he'd given her Beamus instead.

The little man cleared his throat as solemnly as if he were about to present evidence at the king's bench. "Yesterday I followed the lady in question. Her afternoon routine remained as usual."

"More shopping?"

"At the same milliner's establishment." Beamus gave a puzzled frown. "How could one female require so many hats?"

"Obviously you know nothing of women, Beamus."

"Thankfully I can say I do not, sir."

Jared suppressed a smile. He'd always found it amusing and enchanting somehow, Maria's thoroughly feminine adoration of her furbelows and fripperies. She never looked more charming than when her face was framed by a new poke-front bonnet, a saucy bow tied beneath her delicate chin, the ribbons the same hue as her bright blue eyes.

Jared blinked, disgusted with himself. He was surely a fitting candidate for Bedlam when he started daydreaming about Maria and her bonnets. He brushed the image aside, returning to the matter at hand.

"So the contessa visited her milliner's again. What else?" Jared asked impatiently.

"Nothing else, sir. The lady in question passed a quiet day. She did not even set foot out of doors again to attend an evening party. Though before four o'clock, she did send her maid abroad to fetch something. I followed the woman, at a discreet distance, of course."

"Very wise of you," Jared said. He winced as he recalled the buffet Maria's lunatic maid had dealt him on the staircase. Obviously she'd been taking lessons from her mistress. What did those two women do? he wondered. Pop round to Gentleman Jackson's for sparring sessions in between Maria's gown fittings?

"And what was Miss Brewster's errand? Fetching home some toilet water?" Jared asked with a sigh, beginning to feel as if Mr. Beamus might be right. This all did seem to be a monumental waste of money and time.

"Miss Brewster purchased for her mistress one of those pale pink dominoes and a mask," Beamus said.

"A mask?" Jared echoed, tensing.

"Aye, but there's no need to look so alarmed, sir. I'm sure the lady in question has no sinister purpose in mind. There's to be a grand masquerade tonight at Sheffield House. All the quality are going. You must have heard tell of it, sir."

"Yes, I have," Jared said grimly, though his own invitation appeared to have been lost. He would have expected the same thing to have happened to Maria's. It would seem she had every intention of attending, whether invited or not.

He pressed his hand to the bridge of his nose, rubbing his bleary eyes. Maria's comings and goings since returning to town had been mundane until now. She'd not set foot near Miss Lucas. Jared had almost hoped Maria had come to her senses, decided to follow his advice and stay clear of the Duke of Sheffield's ward. He should have known better.

Jared scowled, considering the grim possibilities of the night ahead, wondering just how perilous a masked ball could prove to be, when Mr. Beamus broke into his thoughts.

"Do you wish to continue with my services, sir?"

"No," Jared said slowly. After another frowning moment, he added, "That will not be necessary. You've told me all I needed to know. From here on in, I shall deal with, er . . . *the lady in question* myself."

Jared limped over to a small secretary and drew forth his purse to pay Mr. Beamus his wages. The little man apologized profusely, declaring again that he felt as if he were robbing Sir Jared. But he was quick to pocket the money, looking, Jared thought, like the most cheerful thief he'd ever seen.

But on his way out, Beamus seemed to feel he owed Jared some advice. He turned back on the threshold to say, "It might be presumption on my part, sir. What this affair is all about, I can only hazard a guess."

Beamus heaved a deep sigh. "But a lovely lady like that! Such a sweet, winsome face. Whatever she's done to you, forgive her, sir. If the lady is, shall we say . . . straying, blame the other fellow instead. Blast him to bits."

"Unfortunately I never had the chance," Jared said. "He fell off an Alp."

"Beg pardon, sir?" Beamus was still looking mighty confused when Jared thrust him out the door.

Jared turned and called for Frontenac. He was annoyed when his bellow came out more of a croak, his throat raw from coughing, beginning to affect his voice.

But the Frenchman whipped smartly into the room, awaiting Jared's commands.

"I need you to go out and purchase me a disguise," Jared said.

"A disguise, monsieur?" Frontenac met any order with complete aplomb, but this time he gaped at Jared.

"You know . . . a mask and one of those black domino things."

"What would monsieur require with a mask?" Frontenac asked.

"I'm thinking of taking to the High Toby."

Frontenac primmed his mouth. "I do not believe monsieur should undertake any activity which takes him out of doors tonight. Monsieur already resembles the death's head."

"Merci du compliment," Jared shot back. "Now, will you get the devil out of here and do what I told you?"

"Very well, monsieur. But if monsieur should take the inflammation of the lungs, if he should be dead within the week—"

'Then you warned me. And you can take great satisfaction as usual from being right."

"That is one instance in which I should derive no satisfaction at all, monsieur."

And as Frontenac moved dolefully to don his cloak, hanged if Jared didn't think the fellow really meant it.

The Duke of Sheffield's masquerade proved to be a regal affair, rivaling some of the extravagances of the Prince Regent himself. Champagne flowed from a fountain fashioned to represent a faerie-tale castle, the excess of the bubbling liquid only adding to the aura of reckless merriment.

Throngs of masked revelers danced and flirted with a freedom encouraged by the anonymity of disguise. The lilt of violins, the soft glow of candles, the velvet curtain of night darkening the window-panes ... all contrived to produce an aura of romance and mystery.

Observing the scene through the slits of her own mask, Maria thought she could have done with more romance and far less mystery. If the masquerade offered her the opportunity for concealment, it did the same for her enemy. She tensed at the sight of every dark cape that swirled past, half expecting Sheffield to pounce from its folds, impaling her with the black fury of his eye.

Huddled in the shadows of a large marble pillar, she turned to her nervous companion, a petite shepherdess with soft brown curls. Leaning forward so that her voice could be heard above the hum of voices and the music, Maria said, "We must speak quickly, my dear. Your devil of an uncle may discover me at any moment."

Miss Lucas's eyes blinked with astonishment beneath the satin of her own mask. "Oh, no, Contessa, you are quite mistaken. Uncle is not disguised as a devil tonight."

On some occasions, Maria could find Miss Lucas's childlike manner enchanting. But this wasn't one of them, not when she was so much on edge.

But before Maria was provoked into a testy retort, Miss Lucas relieved some of her apprehension by explaining, "His Grace is not even wearing a mask this evening. You see? He is standing in that far corner over there with the Prince Regent."

Maria hoped the girl was right, but if Sheffield was there, he was hidden by the corpulent prince and several other tall gentlemen.

"I was terrified of being presented to the Prince Regent," Miss Lucas said. "But he was so kind. He congratulated me on my forthcoming marriage and said that he soon must begin calling me 'my lady Pomfrets.' And my fiancé has sent me many presents, including a lovely sapphire ring and—"

But Maria interrupted this artless prattle. "I do trust you remember that along with the lovely ring and title, you are about to acquire a husband. If this is supposed to be a party to honor your engagement, why did this baronet of yours not show himself at last?"

It was cruel perhaps to speak so sharply to the girl. This reminder was all it took to bring tears to Miss Lucas's eyes. "Uncle says that—that Sir Arthur is very shy. But he sent me his portrait. He is not as old as I feared, but oh, Contessa, he is horridly ugly. C-Can you imagine? He wears this great bushy beard and looks as ferocious as a Tartar."

Maria watched in alarm as Miss Lucas drew in a shuddery breath. It would hardly do to have the girl going off into hysterics in the middle of the ballroom, so Maria clasped her hand soothingly.

"You don't have to worry," she said. "You can use the baronet's portrait to frighten away mice, because you're not going to marry him."

Miss Lucas made haste to dab at the tears that were leaving damp splotches on her mask. "I dream every night of Sir Jared Branden charging up the stairs to rescue me. He swoops me up in his arms and carries me off."

Maria made a sound close to a snort. "If Branden ever was obliged to carry you, he'd only complain about your weight."

"You think I'm getting too fat?" Miss Lucas asked anxiously.

"No, I think that Sir Jared is too unromantic. I thought I explained to you that he is not to be depended upon in helping us through this little adventure."

"You did." Miss Lucas sighed. "But I don't see how we are to ever succeed without a gentleman to manage things for us."

Maria pulled a wry face, for she thought, all things considered, she had been managing rather well since their return to London. It had been her clever idea to send messages to Miss Lucas through the milliner they both frequented. And Maria had forged her own card of invitation to the masquerade by copying one that had been sent to a friend.

"I am perfectly capable of arranging for your rescue," she told Miss Lucas rather tartly. "Forget about Sir Jared."

Excellent advice, but unfortunately none that Maria had been able to follow herself. She kept wondering if he was still angry with her. He'd left Silversby Manor without saying another word to her.

Jared's whole attitude had been monstrously unfair. He'd made her feel so wicked and guilty about what had happened in the graveyard that night, almost as though she had been some siren trying to lure him to his doom. But it had been all his doing, embracing her that way.

Jared's kisses always had had the power to render her dizzy, unable to think clearly, to believe in all manner of wildly impossible things . . . like that beneath Jared's cynical facade, there really did exist a man of great and tender heart, of selfless nobility and gallantry.

He was a man of such brilliance, of such a quick mind, at times she'd almost stood a little in awe of him. But for all his cleverness, his rapier wit, he'd never once said the one thing she most wanted to hear, not even after she'd agreed to marry him.

I love you, Maria.

And of a certainty, she wasn't going to hear that now, not after the way she and Jared had parted. There was hardly any reason to be mourning over that. Blame it all on the peculiar influence of St. Valentine's Day. For a brief moment in that churchyard, something had flickered in the ashes of an old romance. Whatever that strange spark had been, far better to leave it buried beneath the ice-cold snow.

Dragging her attention back to Miss Lucas, Maria said, "I have been wracking my brains for a plan to spirit you away."

"Oh, we must be careful! Uncle was so cross when he found me deciphering your secret message last time."

"Was he perfectly horrid to you, child?" Maria squeezed the girl's hand in sympathy.

"Yes." Miss Lucas sniffed. "He scolded me d-dreadfully."

Scolded her? Maria felt some of her sympathy evaporate. She herself had been chased through a graveyard and threatened with a sword stick. But Maria rebuked herself for a want of charity. To a tender-hearted soul like Miss Lucas, a harsh word was like the blow of a lash. Maria ought to remember a time when she was more sensitive herself, when her own papa had had the power to—

But Maria gave herself a brisk mental shake and sought to reassure Miss Lucas. "We will be more careful this time, but I need some information, such as how long do we have before you are to be wed to Sir Arthur. You must find out the duke's plans."

Miss Lucas paled beneath her mask. "Oh, I couldn't. Uncle never tells me anything. I don't even know where the wedding is to take place."

"Then you must employ more subtle means."

Miss Lucas's eyes went wide and very blank. Maria bit back an impatient oath, searching for some way of suggesting to this innocent child the virtues of listening at keyholes.

"Perhaps you could contrive to ... er, overhear

when your uncle is talking to someone else about—"

"Oh, no! I just couldn't do that." Miss Lucas shook her head; her curls even seemed to bounce with horror.

Maria wondered in exasperation if there was anything the girl could do. "You have a right to know something. You are not just a parcel to be moved about at will."

"Well, when my presents came today, my uncle also received a very long letter from Sir Arthur. I noticed His Grace reading it in the study.

"Accidentally," Miss Lucas added hastily. "I wasn't spying."

"Oh, no, I'm dead certain of that," Maria said. "I don't suppose you could try to—" But she checked the suggestion before she finished, realizing the futility of it.

With a sense of grim inevitability, Maria said, "Tell me where the duke's study is."

"It's the first right-hand door leading off the main hall, but what are you going to do, Contessa? I pray that it is nothing His Grace would dislike."

"My dear Miss Lucas," Maria said gently. "If you wish to escape, you are going to have to risk vexing your uncle a little."

"I know, but sometimes I feel it is too bad of me, plotting to run off from my family. I will be in such disgrace."

"That is surely a small price to pay for avoiding a lifetime of misery."

"Yes. Oh yes," Miss Lucas said, but she looked deeply unhappy.

"Courage, child. You must trust me. Everything will come out all right in the end."

She succeeded in coaxing a wan smile from Miss Lucas. Maria was then obliged to take her leave of the girl as Miss Lucas was claimed by her partner for the next dance.

As the young woman disappeared into the crowd, Maria thought she was beginning to comprehend Jared's scorn of the old romantic tales Maria had so cherished. He'd always complained about damsels languishing in the dragon's den, doing nothing but swooning while the poor knight got his derriere scorched, fighting off the fire-breathing monster.

It was dashed unamusing being a hero, Jared had drawled. Much as she hated it, Maria was forced to agree. She felt slightly disgruntled. While Miss Lucas waltzed the night away, she was going to be risking, if not her life, at least considerable embarrassment by searching the duke's study.

But there was no help for it. Although her heart thudded at the prospect ahead of her, Maria made her way through the ballroom. The vast chamber was a crush of masquers, with more arriving by the minute. Maria had almost gained the imposing double doors when her way was barred by a tall man in a black domino.

"Your pardon, sir," she said, trying to skirt round him.

But he quickly outflanked her. "Whither away in such haste, Contessa? The ballroom is behind you."

Startled, Maria glanced up. The voice was strangely husky, but familiar. A dark cape flowed off his broad shoulders. The jaunty tricorn set upon the midnight waves of his hair and the mask that shadowed his lean features gave him the dangerous aura of a highwayman, the sort of bold rogue women gladly handed their diamonds, then hopefully inquired if he wanted them to surrender anything more.

"Branden," she breathed. She thought of trying to pretend he'd mistaken her identity. But as she looked deep into the dark eyes that glittered behind the mask, she realized the absurdity of that.

Fearing that she might have sounded far too glad to see him, she modified her voice to a more formal tone. "Branden! However did you recognize me?"

"I did not for certain. I've been accosting all the blond-haired women this evening. Not a completely disagreeable way to spend one's time."

"I thought you had resolved to eschew the fair sex," she reminded him.

"It's like being thrown from a horse. One has to get back in the saddle sometime. Remarkably, I haven't been leveled by a single woman all night. But then I hadn't run into you yet."

"If you take care not to provoke me, I'll let you remain unscathed." She matched his bantering tone, but her pulse was racing. Only from the shock of seeing him again, she assured herself. She continued, "After what passed between you and the duke, I am astonished that His Grace still sent you an invitation."

"I'm certain I got mine the same place as you did yours—" he began, but was obliged to turn aside, stifling a sudden cough. The spasm caused his shoulders to tremble.

"Jared, are you all right?" she asked, unable to resist laying her hand gently on his arm.

"Your perfume," he rasped. "You—you use too much."

She withdrew her hand at once, stiffening. "Then you should take care not to stand so close if it bothers you. I cannot imagine what you are doing here anyway. Dare one hope you changed your mind about helping Miss Lucas?"

"No, one doesn't dare." He straightened, wiping his handkerchief across his lips, appearing to bring himself under control. "Knowing you would be here tonight, I couldn't resist. It was such a rare entertainment you provided that night in the churchyard. I simply had to catch the next act of this little melodrama."

Sometimes Maria wondered if that was all she had ever been to Jared Branden, a source of amusement.

"As far as you are concerned, sir, the theater is closed." She tried to move away from him, but he linked his arm through hers, steering her towards the door. To anyone else at the ball, he must have appeared quite the gallant, escorting his lady. Only Maria was aware of his tensile grip.

"I came to take you home, Maria," he said, the pleasantness of his tone belied by the steel in his eyes.

"No, you are not," she hissed, struggling to pull free without causing a scene. "Why do you persist in interfering with me, Branden?"

"What am I supposed to do? Let you continue with this foolish intrigue and provoke Sheffield again? I daresay it's my head he will come after. Your ardent lover."

"I might have known that is all you would be worried about."

"Yes, you might have," he replied with a bitter twist of his lips.

A disturbing thought struck Maria, one that caused her to halt in her tracks. Refusing to be budged an inch farther, she looked up at Jared, her eyes narrowing with suspicion. "Exactly how were you so certain I'd be here tonight?"

But he was spared from answering. At that moment a feminine voice called out, "Why, Jared! Is that you, my dearest boy?"

"What the—" Jared's choked exclamation ended in another cough. He stared at a tiny woman rustling towards them, her gown and mask as silvery as her hair.

Maria had never seen Jared look so disconcerted. The elderly woman crept closer, raising her mask to beam at him. She had one of the sweetest faces Maria had ever seen, the lines that feathered her ivory countenance only giving her an appearance of delicate, aged porcelain.

"Don't tell me you don't remember me?" the woman demanded in hurt accents.

Jared stood transfixed a moment more, then limped forward awkwardly to brush a kiss on her cheek. His usual mockery was absent from his voice as he declared, "How could I ever forget my own godmother? It's just that I am surprised to see you, Aunt Clarissa. You never come to London. But it is not time for the unmasking, so you'd best leave this in place."

Godmother? Aunt Clarissa? Maria watched in

fascination as Jared gently helped the older woman restore the mask to her features.

"And how did you know who I was so quickly?" he asked. "I suppose my graceful gait gave me away."

"Foolish boy," she said, reaching up to pat his cheek. "As if I would not always know my favorite godson." The dainty woman turned to acknowledge Maria with a smile. "When I think of all the hours I bounced this great tall fellow on my knee. He used to gurgle and try to nibble on his darling plump little toes."

To Maria's delight, she saw a surge of red creep up Branden's neck.

"Yes, and I'll wager his toes are still just as adorable," she murmured wickedly. The next instant she sucked in her breath as Jared's "darling" toes found her foot and trod down hard.

"So this golden-haired beauty must be your Maria," Jared's godmother cooed. Maria felt her hand being seized in a warm, maternal clasp. "We meet at last, my dear."

His Maria? Maria directed a startled look at Jared. He avoided meeting her eyes.

"Maria, you, of course, have heard me speak of my godmother, my great-aunt, Mrs. Clarissa Branden."

No, she hadn't. But Maria curtsied and smiled. Even after they had become engaged, Jared had never been in any haste to make her known to his family. He spoke so little of his relatives, one would almost have supposed the man to have been an orphan.

Mrs. Branden wagged her finger at Jared. "Such

127

a naughty fellow. Married all these years, and never once have you brought your bride along to visit me."

"M-Married?" Maria gasped.

Jared's godmother leaned closer and whispered, "I'm glad to see you are finally in better health, my dear. It must have been so hard on you, all those confinements."

Confinements? Maria looked to Jared for help in sorting out this bewildering conversation, but he was staring fixedly at the ceiling.

"How are all of the dear sweet babes?" Mrs. Branden asked.

"Well, I—they—" Maria stammered until Jared filled in swiftly.

"They are all well, Aunt Clarissa. We have engaged a new governess, and they are all so busy at lessons, we scarce know they're about."

"Yes, they're practically invisible, in fact," Maria said, then stifled a cry as Jared gave her arm a sharp warning pinch.

"You must all come round to visit me while I am in London. I am staying with Lord and Lady Jeffries and— Oh, dear, I see another old acquaintance beckoning to me. What silly things these masquerades are. As if one still doesn't know who everyone is."

With many apologies and wringing promises from Jared he would bring Maria to wait upon her immediately, Mrs. Branden fluttered off again.

Maria cast a fulminating glance at Jared. For once, the man had the decency to look abashed, but before she could question Jared, he gripped her arm once more and propelled her from the ball-room.

It was only when they reached the relative quiet of the balcony that overlooked the stairs sweeping down to the hall below that Maria dug in her heels. She turned on him and demanded, "Jared Branden! What sort of faradiddles have you been telling that poor woman?"

"You mustn't mind my great-aunt Clarissa. She's a charming woman, but a little . . . vague. I wrote her years ago about you and our engagement. But she never seemed able to absorb the fact that I had never actually gotten married. So after a time, I simply gave over the effort to explain to her."

"And our *children?*"

Jared winced. "Well, we could hardly have been wed all those years without producing any off-spring." He gave a sheepish smile. "I'm afraid you've had a rather hard time of it, my dear. Seven confinements."

"Seven!" For a moment Maria was tempted to ask him if she had been delivered of boys or girls. Then she brought herself sharply to her senses. "This is completely infamous, even for you, Branden! How could you play such a horrid jest on that sweet old lady?"

"It wasn't a jest."

"What was it then?"

He spun away from her, using the dim light of the landing to shadow his features as effectively as the mask. "My aunt Clarissa used to slip me guineas under the sealing wax of her letters when I was a boy, sent me books on my birthday. She's the only one of my relatives whose opinion of me I have ever given a damn about.

"It was easier somehow to let her believe that I was this contented squire raising children in the country instead of wasting my life in London, raising hell."

"But how could you possibly have maintained such a hoax all these years?"

He shrugged. "Since my great-uncle died, my godmother has lived a quiet life in Yorkshire. She very seldom ventures abroad unless it is some great event like a coronation or royal wedding. That is why I was so startled to see her."

"But surely your own family must have betrayed you."

"Not necessarily. It is as I always told you. We Brandens are not a warm and communicative lot such as your own family was."

"Y-e-ss." Maria lowered her eyes. It was difficult to remain too indignant with Branden for his distortion of the truth when she knew she was guilty of more than a few Banbury tales of her own.

"You never actually met any of my father's side of the family," Jared added. "Or perhaps you'd better understand."

"So you no longer have much contact with any of them yourself?" she asked.

"Very little except the infrequent letter. My father, as you know, is dead. My brother George, after having covered himself with glory at Waterloo, is now making his fortune in India. Daniel is off sailing around the world again, gathering material for another of those travel books he writes. And my oldest brother is buried in the family plot, a statue erected to his military exploits."

Jared pulled a wry face. "But I daresay even he is happy. Stanway always wanted to grow up to be a monument."

"And you, Jared . . . are you happy?"

Maria did not know what possessed her to ask such a thing, but in some odd way, Jared did not seem to be quite himself tonight. He leaned up against the banister, appearing grateful for its support. She wondered if he might have been drinking too much. It was not a welcome supposition.

But he forced himself erect, saying in his usual rallying tones, "Am I happy? Oh, prodigiously so. I've won large sums at Crockford's three nights running. What more bliss can a man ask for?"

Maria sighed. Why did she trouble herself to worry about the man?

"I'm sorry, Maria, if that business with my godmother caused you any embarrassment. I suppose if she's going to be traipsing about town, I'd better make another effort to tell her the truth before she hears it from someone else."

"I suppose you'd better," Maria agreed. But she didn't know what was wrong with her. She should have been demanding Jared tell his aunt the truth at once. Instead the prospect filled her with a strange sorrow and regret.

"I believe I rather envy your godmother," she said.

"Envy Aunt Clarissa? In God's name, why?"

"I never knew there was anyone whose good opinion you valued."

"That's where you are quite mistaken. I—" He

took a step away, clearing his throat. "You must have noticed how I dote upon my dear uncle Charles."

"Poor Lord Brixted. I don't know what you did to vex him so over Valentine's Day. I have a feeling you teased him shamefully about something."

"He's an old fool."

"Not so very old. And still a fine figure of a man."

"He wears corsets!"

"For all I know, so do you."

Jared's lips curled in a wicked smile. "I'd be happy to show you otherwise, my dear. I believe I was about to escort you home before we were interrupted."

Maria had been on the verge of smiling back, but she curbed her imprudent response to Jared's teasing. His words only served as a reminder of the dispute they had been having before his aunt had arrived.

"There is no need for an armed guard to remove me from the premises," she said. "I was on the verge of leaving anyway."

But Jared was not so easily fooled or gotten rid of. He trailed her to the hall below. Maria bit her lip in vexation. The servants were busy with arriving and departing guests. The opportunity for slipping unnoticed into Sheffield's study was too perfect to be missed.

Turning, she murmured to Jared, "Be a dear and have my carriage sent for. I have to step into that parlor for a moment to retrieve something that was left."

Not giving him a chance to protest, Maria whisked away from him. Acting as casually as she could, she sauntered over to the door Miss Lucas had told her about.

Inching it open a crack, Maria peered inside. It was Sheffield's study, all right, the room dark, forbidding, but empty. A fire that burned low in the grate seemed to cast an eerie glow over the outline of a massive desk. But she had braved the dragon's flames before, Maria thought, taking a nervous breath.

"What are you doing?"

Jared's voice so close to her nearly startled her into a shriek. She glanced over her shoulder to find Jared directly behind her, scowling. One would think the man did not trust her an inch out of his sight.

Placing a cautioning finger against her lips, Maria slipped inside the room. Jared followed her.

"Damn it, Maria. This isn't any parlor. What mischief—"

"Shh!" she hissed. "Close the door, and if you're going to be my lookout, you'd best lower your voice."

"Your lookout!" Jared choked, then covered his mouth, stifling another coughing spell. Apparently the air in Sheffield's study didn't agree with him any more than her perfume did.

Maria marched boldly over to Sheffield's desk and started to yank open the topmost drawer. But before she could proceed any further, Jared was there, forcing it closed. "How the deuce does something of yours come to be in Sheffield's desk?"

"I didn't say I was searching for anything that I left."

Jared swore roundly. "I vow if Sheffield doesn't

strangle you, I'll do it myself, woman. What are you trying to do now, get yourself brought up on charges for attempted theft? That silly girl is not worth these risks, Maria."

"Is there anything you do think is worth the risk?"

"I better not answer that. You just might want to hit me again."

"I will if you don't get out of my way—" she began, then blinked, her heart beginning to beat faster. Beneath Jared's arm she could see that what looked like a letter had been left lying carelessly on top of the desk, the lines of the paper crossed and recrossed with a spidery handwriting. Could the luck be with her for once? Could it really be this easy?

"Look, Jared," she cried, forgetting that he was not exactly her eager coconspirator. "That might be the letter Miss Lucas told me about."

Over his muttered protests, she lit a candle and placed it on the desk, shifting the first sheet more into the light. The inked scrawl was difficult to read, and what she could decipher only caused Maria to purse her lips. She checked the last page for the signature.

"This is definitely from Miss Lucas's baronet. But how very disappointing," she said. "It is full of nothing but boring details about marriage settlements."

"What did you expect? It is only natural when a man is about to be married."

"I don't recall you ever going on about such things when we were engaged."

"That is because I was a fool," Jared said irritably. He turned aside to sneeze into his handkerchief. "Now, are you quite finished, Maria? What the deuce did you hope to find in here anyway?"

"I was looking for some mention of when or where this infamous wedding is to take place so that I . . ." Maria trailed off at the sound of a masculine voice just outside the door.

She exchanged a startled glance with Jared. The door handle turned, but only opened partly as the person without paused to exchange another word with someone else in the hall.

Maria dropped the letter, her heart pounding. But before she could do anything more, Jared moved swiftly. He plunked down onto the duke's chair, pulled Maria into his lap, and began kissing her hard.

She struggled, voicing a muffled protest just as the door swung open.

A bewigged footman in satin livery crossed the threshold, only to draw up short, gasping.

Jared relaxed his hold on Maria enough to glare. "Was there something you wanted?"

"Uh—n-no sir, that is—"

"Then go away. You can see this room is occupied."

Before Maria could get out a word, Jared's mouth covered hers in a kiss that was passionate enough to have sent a dozen footmen retreating in horrified embarrassment.

Maria heard the door close. "J-Jared, he's gone," she managed to get out. "That was excessively clever of—oh!" she cried as Jared kissed her again.

He appeared to have quite forgotten the original purpose of the ploy. As his lips sought hers, hot, hungry, seeking, Maria stood in danger of forgetting herself.

Burying her fingers in his hair, she returned his embrace with equal fervor, the heated feel of his mouth, his skin, sending shivers of ecstasy coursing through her.

But gradually it became borne in on her that something was very wrong. She wrenched back enough to gasp, "Branden, you're burning up."

"You finally noticed," he murmured, his lips blazing a trail of fire along the column of her neck.

Splaying her hands on his chest, she held him at bay. "No, I mean you truly are on fire." Quickly undoing the strings, she removed his mask and placed her hand to his forehead.

Jared tried to stay the gesture by kissing her fingertips, but she persisted, placing the back of her hand against his flushed cheeks.

"I think you have a fever." With some alarm, she also noticed how haggard he looked in the flickering candlelight. "My God, what have you been doing to yourself?"

"Nothing." He thrust her off his knee, looking annoyed. "I wish everyone would stop taking such a keen interest in my health."

Groping for his mask, he jammed it awkwardly back in place. "Now, if you are quite finished here, perhaps we can leave."

Maria wasn't, but suddenly the thought of searching Sheffield's study no longer seemed of such importance. Deny it though he would, it was obvious Jared was alarmingly ill. Maria berated herself for not having noticed it sooner.

Her one thought became getting the man to go

home, go to his bed. She would pretend to leave herself if she had to, and then slip back later.

Unfortunately, the line of departing guests calling for their wraps and carriages had lengthened. They faced a full half-hour wait in the drafty hall. Maria tried not to irritate Jared by hovering, but she could not help notice a shiver course through him, and his mask bore damp patches of sweat.

She nearly cried out in relief when her own carriage drew up to the doorstep. But to her dismay, after helping her inside, Jared closed the door and prepared to step back.

She lowered the glass and thrust her head out the coach window. "Jared, did you come by hansom?"

"What an embarrassing question. Do you think I'm not in funds enough to keep my own coach?"

"Don't be absurd. Let me take you back to your lodgings."

He gave a wan smile. "I've never met any woman full of so many delightfully improper suggestions."

"Jared, please. Truly you are not well."

"You need not concern yourself, Titania. I'm fine."

He was still assuring her this was so when his knees sagged out from under him and he toppled to the pavement.

"Jared!" Maria screamed.

Chapter 7

She was calling his name, but he couldn't find her.

Jared groaned, his head tossing on a pillow soaked with sweat; his entire world seemed to be on fire.

Flame and smoke. It was everywhere, belching from the mouths of a hundred cannons whose terrifying roar filled his ears, all but obliterating the softer, gentler sound.

Jared.

"Maria," he moaned. He coughed until his throat felt raw, the acrid smoke scorching his lungs as he strove to see through the thick haze. "Where are you?"

His only answer was the thunder of gunfire, the screams of dying men. Then in the distance he could see it, untouched by all this madness erupting around him, the serene beauty of an English country church. Upon the steps, waiting for him, stood a maiden all in white, her golden hair flowing to her waist, a crown of flowers adorning her pale white brow. A bit of heaven in the midst of hell.

"Maria!" He staggered towards her through the

thick, choking smoke, the hail of cannon fire. Another shot rang out and he knew he'd been hit.

But even in the midst of his fever-tossed delirium, Jared realized that something wasn't right. His leg . . . he had taken the shot in his leg. Yet it was his chest that burned, a searing pain in the region of his heart.

Choking, he struggled to go on. Hands attempted to restrain him. Even though they were cool, gentle, he fought against them, forcing himself forward.

The church. He had to get to the church. He could see Maria standing there, shielding her eyes as she searched the distance.

"Maria . . . coming," he muttered. "Wait for me."

Yet the harder he tried, the farther away the church seemed to be. Maria turned away with a sad shake of her head.

"No! Don't go!" he cried, but the church was vanishing, fading before his eyes into the mists of battle. His knees sagged beneath him and he fell, clutching his chest.

To his horror, he felt as though his heart were being torn from him, but when his hands came away, they clutched only a heart made of paper. The lacy valentine shredded to bits in his hand, the pieces borne away on the wind.

A shuddering sob wracked through him, then the hands came again, the touch upon his cheek calm and soothing.

Through his raging fever, Jared forced his eyes open, tried to focus upon the face hovering over him, the face of an angel, her golden hair a veil of light, a thousand spring mornings glowing in the soft hue of her eyes.

He clutched at her arm. "Maria, don't . . . don't leave me."

"I won't. I'm here, love," she promised him, her voice low, sweet, and sad. "Now, please, Jared. Try to sleep."

With a deep sigh, he relaxed beneath her caress. His eyes fluttered closed as she stroked his brow. The sounds of battle faded as he allowed his maiden of light to lead him into the blessed darkness.

The next time his eyes opened, the smoke, the battlefield, had faded. It was the pearly light of day that misted his vision, a satin coverlet tucked up to his chin. He clung to the ends of it like a storm-tossed ship seeking an anchor. The urge to drift back to sleep was strong. He felt so weak, exhausted. But he fought against it, struggling through a fog of confusion until he was able to focus on his surroundings.

Damn, he thought, stifling a groan. He must've really shot the cat this time. This was becoming a dangerous habit of his, waking in strange places with no notion where he was.

He was lying pillowed in the downy softness of a canopy bed, hung with ivory satin embroidered in gold. The light, airy textures of the room beyond almost hurt his eyes, the wallpaper fashioned after a Chinese pattern, the delicate chairs and wardrobe painted to simulate bamboo. The entire bedchamber had an aura of subtle femininity, the mystery and allure of an Oriental harem girl.

And huddled on a settee near the bed slept

Jared's silent angel. He turned his head on the pillow and hardly dared blink for fear this apparition would vanish. Maria's golden lashes rested against her cheeks, her head drooping against a velvet pillow, her bare feet peeking out from beneath the hem of her simple sprigged muslin gown. Her hair tumbled about her shoulders in golden disarray, doing more to cover her than the cashmere shawl which had pooled to the carpet.

It was as breathtaking as discovering a faerie asleep beneath one's rosebushes, all the legend and magic Jared had never allowed himself to believe in. But this particular faerie looked pale, blue circles of exhaustion beneath her eyes.

Jared longed for nothing more than to go to her, gather her into his arms. He cursed the weakness that kept him chained to the bed. Where was he and what was Maria doing here? Fragments of memory sifted through his head ... Sheffield's masquerade, kissing Maria in the study, the cold, hard feel of a cobblestone street, a jolting carriage ride, his head pillowed in Maria's lap.

With supreme effort, Jared raised himself up onto one elbow only to fall back against the mattress. The noise, slight as it was, startled Maria awake.

She sat bolt upright, looking as frightened and disoriented as a child rudely awakened. Then her gaze locked on him, a radiant smile curving her lips.

"Jared. You—you're awake. And you're alive."

He tried to smile back, but his lips cracked painfully and his answering retort came out as no more than a croak. Maria staggered from the settee, her bare feet padding across the Oriental carpet as she hastened to a small table to pour him a glass of water.

Coming back to the bedside, she slipped one hand gently beneath his neck, raising him up enough to guide the glass to his lips. It was only then that Jared realized how thirsty he was. He drank greedily, the cool liquid sliding down his parched throat.

Sinking back against the pillows with a deep sigh, he managed to rasp, "Am I alive? How very . . . disappointing. I'd hoped this might be heaven."

"No, only my bedchamber in my house in Mayfair."

"I've been in your bed and . . . can't remember a thing. Incredible. I'm exhausted. You must not have been very gentle . . . with me."

Color flooded into her cheeks. "You were deathly ill with a fever, Jared. How can you make such horrid jests?"

He jested because he was flat on his back before her, helpless and vulnerable. It was obvious she'd been nursing him like a sick child, and not over anything as grand as a wound, only a damned chill. He'd swooned in her arms like a girl. Never in his life had he been further from the heroic visions Maria so cherished.

Drawing in a painful breath, Jared made an effort to rise, at least to a sitting position. The coverlet fell away, exposing the dark, matted hairs of his chest.

"Oh, no, you mustn't try to get up," Maria said, pressing her hands to his bare shoulders. In that instant he realized he was naked beneath the sheets.

Maria appeared suddenly conscious of it as well. As he sank against the pillows, she drew back, looking awkward and embarrassed.

"Have—Have you been sitting up with me all night?" Jared asked hoarsely, tugging the coverlet up to his chin.

"Most of it. You were delirious, but the doctor said you'd be all right after we broke your fever. But then you slept and slept until I was almost afraid that—that you never meant to wake."

"What time is it now?"

"Nearly evening."

"I've been here a night and a day?" He winced. "Damn it, Maria. Why'd you bring me to your place?"

"What was I supposed to do, leave you lying in the street?"

"You could've run over me or dumped me on my own doorstep. I know your charitable nature, but even you can't go about dragging home unconscious men. Do you want to set every tongue in London to wagging?"

"I've been properly chaperoned. Your godmama is here, too."

"Aunt Clarissa?"

"She was coming out of Sheffield House when you collapsed. The poor woman was beside herself. What else could I do but bring her along? She's been a great support to me. She's probably downstairs in the parlor even now, knitting socks."

"Good Lord. For me?" Jared groaned.

"No. For our eldest son. The one who's away at school."

When Jared stared at her, she spread her hands in a helpless gesture. "I also seem to be having difficulty clarifying the situation to your aunt Clarissa."

Jared frowned, resting one hand across his eyes. "I'll straighten out the entire matter as soon I can speak with her."

"Don't worry about that now. I can pretend a while longer."

"Is that why you put me in your bed?"

She took so long in replying, he shifted his hand to look at her. She squirmed with embarrassment. "Well, no . . . it just sort of happened. It seemed the perfect place. My bed is the most comfortable, and this is the largest room." She moistened her lips and glanced away. "And you must stay here until you are quite well again."

"Oh, I've never been in any hurry to quit the bed of a beautiful woman," he drawled. But he thought that he would far rather be anyplace else than here in Maria's bedchamber. His mission last night had been to keep the woman out of mischief, not draw her further into it. He was damned if he wanted to be next on the list of Maria's tender-hearted quests, another of her strays.

It was only worse when she moved about the room, in the manner of a brisk nursery-room governess, plumping his pillows, adjusting the curtains to shield his eyes from the light, fetching more water to bathe his face.

He tensed as she bent over the bed, golden strands of her hair whispering like silk against his bare shoulder. Her hand was soft and gentle as she brushed the hair back from his eyes, applied the cooling cloth to his brow.

He was half-dead. She shouldn't have been able to fill him with such untoward longings. But he supposed he would have to be all dead before Maria's beauty ceased to have effect upon him. Fighting against the stirring of desire, he sought to stare past her, concentrate upon the objects of the room.

His gaze came to rest upon a small framed por trait resting on the satinwood table by the bedside. Mocking dark eyes set above a sweep of mustache stared back at him.

"That's your Count Macaroni?" he asked glumly.

Maria followed the line of his gaze. "Yes, that's my Roberto."

Jared frowned and turned his head the other way. "I think I'm about to have a relapse."

Usually such remarks would have instantly aroused Maria's ire. But all she said was, "I'll take the miniature away if you like."

She lifted the oval frame, hugging it against her breasts in a way that only added to Jared's depression of spirits. The handsome face in the painting made him more keenly aware of his own disheveled state. He rubbed his hand along the rough stubble of his beard.

"I must look like the devil."

"Yes, but then you always do. After you've rested a bit more and managed to take a little tea or gruel, I'll send Frontenac to you."

"He's here, too?" Jared sighed. "Then you'd bet ter go get some rest yourself, Titania, and send him in at once. The fellow will be fair bursting to say, 'I told you so.'"

"Frontenac has been very concerned about you, as we all have been. He helped me to take care of you when you were delirious."

Jared shifted uncomfortably, a new and disturbing thought striking him. "Delirious? You mean . . . Was I thrashing about?"

"Oh, like a tiger."

"Did I . . . That is, I suppose I was also raving?"

"A little."

Apprehension pressed down upon Jared, but he managed to jest, "So now you know all my deepest, darkest secrets?"

"At least one of them."

"Damnation! Which one?"

Maria's lips curled into a half smile.

"You really don't wear corsets." And with that she turned and fled from the room.

Leaning up against the closed door, Maria experienced a fleeting satisfaction. It wasn't often that one could put Jared Branden to the blush.

But her smile swiftly faded and she trembled. After a night and day of hovering over Jared, watching, hoping, praying, she suddenly realized how drained she was and how frightened she had been.

The doctor had been reassuring, telling her that Jared had a hearty constitution, despite the fact he'd been doing his obvious best to destroy it. All the same, during that long first night, Maria had despaired of his fever ever breaking. The throes of the agony that bound him seemed as though they would never set him free. He had tossed so violently, crying out, that at times it had taken the combined strength of both herself and his valet to restrain him.

From the fragments Jared had muttered, she had been able to tell that his delirium had taken him back to some private hell, the plains of the battlefield where he had nearly lost his leg. But only certain words had stood out clear, uttered with a pathos that had been enough to break her heart.

Maria . . . don't leave me.

Jared had never addressed her with such emotion, as though his very soul cried out to hers. If Jared had spoken so to her on a cold winter's afternoon ten years ago, then perhaps . . .

Maria looked down at the portrait she had painted of her Count Roberto and sighed. Then perhaps things might have turned out very differently.

She remembered so clearly that bitter January day, herself seated primly upon the settee in the drawing room of her home, Jared pacing before the fire, restless and impatient with her.

"Our engagement is at an end, Jared," she had repeated, swallowing hard over the words that came so difficult for her.

"Why?" he had demanded. "Is it because of something your father has said to you? I know he has never exactly seemed warm to the notion of my marrying you, but—"

"Oh, no. It has nothing to do with Papa." Maria hung her head. If Jared only knew . . . Her Papa was never warm about anything, including his only child. She swallowed again and continued, "It must be as painfully obvious to you as it is to me. We simply do not suit."

"We're not a deck of playing cards, Maria. There

147

are bound to be these little set-tos between any couple."

"Little set-tos! We disagree on everything that is important."

"Not on one thing." Smiling confidently, Jared moved to take her into his arms.

Hard as it was, she whisked herself away from him. She could not allow herself to be swayed or confused by Jared's kiss, something the man was far too good at doing. "We can't spend the rest of our lives locked in an embrace."

"Why not?"

"Because as soon as our lips part and either of us can speak, we usually start quarreling again. No two people were ever more unlike except for . . ."

She trailed off. She had almost said, *except for my own parents*. But she had fed both Jared and herself so many pretty lies about her mother and father's faerie-tale marriage, it was too late to deal with the truth now.

"You are only having an attack of prenuptial nerves." Jared shrugged. "You'll get over that as soon as you become Mrs. Jared Branden and have the pleasure of spending my fortune. That is, as soon as I acquire a fortune for you to spend."

"Jared, please listen," she whispered, fighting back tears. "We can't go through with this. I don't believe your attachment for me is strong enough. We'd only end up hating each other someday."

Instead of seeking to reassure her, he moved to gather up his hat and riding gloves. "It is best we were married as soon as possible. I spoke to the reverend of your local church. We can be wed on St. Valentine's Day. All Fools' Day might be more appropriate, but you surely would not wish to wait that long."

He seized her hand and planted a light, teasing kiss on her fingertips, but his jaw had been flexed at a most stubborn angle.

"I shall meet you at the church vestibule at ten o'clock."

"I won't be there, Jared."

But he made her a smart bow and left. It had been obvious he hadn't believed her, hadn't heard a word that she'd said. At the time, Maria had ascribed his behavior to obstinacy, pure male arrogance.

But now those agonized words he'd whispered in the depths of his fever echoed again through her head. *Maria, don't leave me.*

Was it possible she'd made a great mistake, that Jared really had cared for her to a depth she'd never imagined? Or was she imagining things now, refining too much upon tormented words spoken in a fever?

After all these years, what odds did it make? She had pursued her own life, and Jared had pursued his. They both had survived the broken engagement of their youth. With the coldness, the loneliness, she'd known in her own childhood, she still needed the kind of love and assurance that Branden seemed incapable of giving. He used his wit like a rapier, his teasing smile like a shield, and there was no getting close to him. What was to be done with a man who only revealed his heart when he was wracked with fever? One couldn't keep him constantly ill.

No, Maria reflected sadly. Nothing had changed.

Nothing except her growing tendency to sigh over the past and gather wool when she should be concentrating upon other things.

Still hugging Roberto's portrait to her chest, she went to seek out Frontenac and send him in to his master. After that, she glided down to the front parlor, where Jared's godmother awaited her.

The tiny Englishwoman looked rather strange seated upon one of Maria's exotic Egyptian-style chairs with its arms carved into snarling lions. But she sat placidly knitting, squinting at her stitches in the fading evening light.

As Maria bustled forward to fetch some candles for her, the old woman looked up with an anxious smile.

"Jared has awakened at last?"

"Yes," Maria said. "I'm sure by this time he is bellowing for a beefsteak and his shaving brush."

Aunt Clarissa heaved a deep sigh, then went back to counting her stitches. "I told you how it would be, my dear. Though he gave us a dreadful fright, I was certain Jared would be all right. Branden men have always been a tough lot, though nary a one of them ever possessed the sense to keep to their beds when ill. I am sure you will notice some of the same hardheaded tendencies in your own boys as they grow older."

"Ye-e-ess," Maria agreed uncomfortably. She realized she still carried Roberto's picture, and set it upon the mantel while she arranged a branch of candles closer to Aunt Clarissa's elbow.

Aunt Clarissa set her knitting aside, coaxing Maria to sit upon the sofa, patting her hand in motherly fashion. "You may bear me company for a moment, child, then you must go and get some rest yourself. I can see that roguish nephew of mine has given you a bad time of it, though I daresay it was much worse when the boy went off and got himself wounded fighting that monster Bonaparte."

"Oh, yes, that must have been dreadful. I—I mean I remember. It was."

Maria squirmed. This was a terrible thing, practicing deception on this elderly lady. But Branden had begun it, and it was up to him to end it. Looking into Aunt Clarissa's vague, sweet blue eyes, Maria did not envy him the task.

"It surprised me a great deal when I heard Jared had gone into the military," Aunt Clarissa said. "He was always such a bookish little waif, quite out of step with the rest of the army-mad Branden family."

Maria blinked in astonishment at this description. She had difficulty imagining Branden as any kind of waif, bookish or otherwise.

"I daresay he simply succumbed to the lure of a smart red coat at last. Trying to impress you, no doubt, my dear."

"M-Me?"

"I remember the things he used to write me when he was courting you. He was always concerned you did not find him daring enough. Foolish of him, wasn't it?"

"Very foolish," Maria agreed faintly. There had been many things she had thought that Jared was not, not tender enough, not romantic enough. But daring? The mad neck-or-nothing way he had been wont to ride his horse had always brought her heart to her throat. But he no longer took such risks anymore, he said. Because of his leg.

That prospect should have given her nothing but relief. Instead it made her rather sad.

"So the military tradition in Jared's family was very strong?" Maria ventured.

"Oh, my, yes." Clarissa gave a silvery laugh. "The only ones who never seemed to hear the call of the drum were Jared and my own Henry. But the rest of the Branden men lived with the hope of going out in a blaze of glory. Jared must have told you how both his father and grandfather died on battlefields. He never knew either of them, poor boy. I suppose that is why he grew up adoring his oldest brother, Stanway."

Stanway? Maria nearly choked. The brother she had only ever heard Jared refer to as Stanway the Idiot? The same Stanway who had wanted to grow up to be a monument?

"I'm sure Jared must have been devastated when Stanway died at Waterloo."

"Indeed," Maria murmured. She was beginning to wonder if she knew anything about Jared Branden at all. She longed to press the elderly woman with dozens of questions. But it must seem odd enough already, how little Maria understood about the man she was supposed to have been married to these past ten years.

Yet with no prodding, Aunt Clarissa settled back in her chair and continued. She seemed to take great pleasure in her reminiscences. "Jared was always very fond of my late husband, his great-uncle Henry. They were so alike, those two. At times I found my dear Henry a most aggravating, frustrating man. I daresay you often feel the same about Jared."

"Often," Maria agreed heartily.

"He teases when you desire him to be serious?"

"All the time."

"He hardly ever says the romantic words you wish to hear?"

"Almost never!"

"And even when he does perform some noble action, he must always play the cynic, turning everything into a jest?"

"Constantly," Maria cried, amazed by the depth of the old lady's perception.

"And yet despite the lack of pretty words, he is there when you need him most?"

"Well, he—he—" Maria paused, a little stunned by the realization. "Yes, I suppose Jared has come frequently to my rescue, although he complains most bitterly."

"Just like my Henry." Clarissa nodded and smiled. She gave Maria's hand another squeeze. "Patience, my dear. It takes a deal of persistence to find the love and tenderness these Branden men keep hidden beneath their tarnished armor, but the effort is worth it.

"However, I'm sure I don't need to tell you all these things about your own husband." There was suddenly a look of such shrewdness in Clarissa's vague eyes that Maria tensed.

She knows everything, Maria thought, starting to blush, preparing to stammer out apologies and explanations.

But the keen look vanished so swiftly, Maria could not be sure that she hadn't imagined it.

The old lady arose from her chair, shaking out her skirts. She further disconcerted Maria by gliding over to the mantel to inspect the miniature that Maria had painted of Roberto.

Jared's godmother would be bound to ask who it was, and what was Maria going to say? A brother? A cousin? While Maria's mind raced, thinking up an identity for the man in the portrait, Aunt Clarissa confounded her by saying, "What a remarkable likeness of Jared. I didn't know he ever had grown a mustache."

"He—he didn't. . . . That isn't . . ." Maria stammered. "I—I mean he did for a while, but—but then he shaved it off."

"How fortunate for you, my dear. I never liked facial hair on a man. So scratchy."

Aunt Clarissa turned away from the portrait, and Maria breathed a deep sigh. The old woman must be dreadfully nearsighted, to have thought she perceived Branden's likeness beneath the fierce mustache of Maria's Italian count.

Clarissa crossed the room to brush a light kiss on Maria's cheek. "I've kept you here with my foolish chatter long enough when you are so spent. I intend to have a bit of supper in my room and retire early myself. You should go to bed, my dear."

Maria promised Clarissa that she would, but long after the older woman had gone, Maria lingered in the parlor.

She whisked over to the mantel and snatched up the portrait, holding it close to her eyes. She didn't know why Clarissa's mistake should disturb her, but it did.

It was a likeness of Roberto, the Conte di

Montifiori Vincerone. Maria had painted it herself. She ought to know whom it was meant to represent. But the longer she stared, the more uncertain she became. Those eyes that looked back at her, those familiar teasing dark eyes, the eyes of . . . No, it couldn't be!

Maria replaced the portrait with shaking hands. Perhaps it was not Clarissa Branden who was the nearsighted one after all.

Over the next few days of Jared's recovery, Maria avoided being alone with him, leaving his care mostly to his devoted valet and his godmother. She confined her services to ransacking her library for books that might please him and conferring with her cook about delicacies to tempt his appetite. It had been one thing to hover at Jared's bedside when he had been feverish, asleep. But Maria could not continue attending him when he was no longer so vulnerable, so helpless.

Propriety, Maria assured herself.

Cowardice, a voice inside her whispered.

That nagging voice persisted in haunting her through the third evening of Jared being an unwilling guest in her house. Aunt Clarissa had, as usual, retired early, leaving Maria lingering in the tiny room that served as both library and back parlor.

Balanced on a stepladder, Maria rummaged about on the top shelf of the bookcase, uncovering a volume that brought a wry smile to her lips. Homer's *The Odyssey.* All those years ago, she had remembered to send Jared his ring back, but had forgotten to give him the book he had lent her. She doubted that he had cared anything for the priceless band of diamonds and sapphires, but she was astonished he hadn't turned up on her doorstep, demanding his precious Homer. She would have to summon Frontenac to take the book up to Jared at once and—

But that niggling voice inside of her whispered again, *Coward!*

As Maria carefully descended the stepladder, she sighed, unable to deny it any longer. It was true. She was having difficulty facing Jared since her realization about the portrait. Part of her still wished to explain away the subtle resemblance to Jared. It was mere coincidence. But another part of her had no choice but to acknowledge that even when she had been painting her beloved Roberto, she had not fully relinquished her memories of Jared Branden.

For years she had deluded herself that everything had ended between them on that Valentine's Day she had failed to join Jared at St. Stephen's Church. But now she feared that nothing had ever been resolved, that somehow she and Jared were an unfinished story, a play that had yet to see its final act.

That last scene might well be played out tomorrow. Jared was well enough that Maria knew he would insist upon returning to his own lodgings. She sensed that his going would put more than the distance of a few London streets between them. Those few times she had peeked into Jared's room, he had been as awkward with her as she was with him. She knew what was wrong. Jared had always loathed appearing vulnerable to anyone, and Maria had seen him at his most helpless. He was closing her out again, and with more finality than he had ever done before.

Tomorrow they would once more be two people going their separate ways, Jared back to his clubs, his gaming, and his sports, she to her own round of social engagements and her schemes to help poor Miss Lucas.

They would bid each other good-bye in her parlor. Maria would remark that he was not well enough, that he should remain a few days longer. Jared would firmly refuse. He might warn her again about meddling with the Duke of Sheffield's affairs, and she would politely thank him for his solicitude, but tell him he must no longer concern himself. And perhaps this time he wouldn't.

She and Jared Branden actually being civil to each other. Lord, what a strange and melancholy prospect. Maria's lips quirked into a rueful smile. She wiped away the light coating of dust from the ancient volume and told herself to stop being such a fool.

No matter what had passed between them, she had known Jared far too long to start behaving as stiff and bashful with him as a schoolroom miss. There was no reason she should not march straight upstairs and return his book to him tonight.

Such a simple errand. Maria was at a loss to understand why her pulse should skitter so as she left the library. By the time she reached the upper landing, her heart was fair drumming in her ears.

When she raised her knuckles to knock at Jared's door, it annoyed her to see that her hand was less than steady. Jared had continued to occupy her own bedchamber during his convalescence, while

Maria had insisted upon taking one of the guest rooms. It had been one of the few arguments she had ever won with the man.

She rapped lightly and heard Jared's curt voice bidding her enter. As she opened the door, she expected to find Jared propped up in bed, his valet in attendance.

The light of a single candle on the bedside table revealed nothing but rumpled bedclothes. There was no sign of the patient or his valet. Her gaze tracking about the room, she saw Jared's shadow reflected by the roaring blaze on the hearth. Clad in his dressing gown, he stood by one of the windows that fronted the square, looking out. The lacy curtain billowed with a stiff breeze that caused the candle to flicker.

"Frontenac," Jared growled, without looking around. "I told you I didn't want to be disturbed anymore tonight. If you've brought me another of your devilish possets, you'd best take it away again before I force you to drink it yourself."

Maria swallowed. This was more than she had bargained for, finding Jared alone and prowling about the room, as restless and untamed as any great jungle cat.

He didn't wish to be disturbed. She ought to simply slip from the room. Instead she found herself softly closing the door, unable to tear her eyes away from him.

The glow from the hearth illuminated his broad shoulders, the wine-colored satin of his dressing gown, the ebony waves of his hair. Maria caught a glimpse of bare feet, muscular calves, and she couldn't help recalling what an embarrassed

Frontenac had confided to her that first night when Jared's fever had raged.

"The master can never rest easy sleeping with any manner of clothing on, not even when he's well."

Maria had tried to modestly avert her eyes while Frontenac had stripped Jared of all garments. But it had been difficult with Jared thrashing about so. She could not help but see flashes of the magnificent wall of his chest, the soft sprinkling of dark hairs, the taut plane of his stomach, the strong, sinewy look of his thighs, and—and other masculine accoutrements.

It was shameful of her, with Jared unconcious, raging with fever. She shouldn't have been noticing such things, but she couldn't seem to help reflecting. Jared Branden certainly would not have been a disappointment to any bride on her wedding night.

Maria's cheeks fired with the remembrance. She was seeking some graceful way to stop ogling Jared and make him aware of her presence when he suddenly spun about as if startled.

She wasn't sure what had alerted him. Perhaps she had unknowingly released a tremulous sigh. Now he was staring just as intently at her.

"Maria," he murmured in surprise.

She clutched the book to her bosom like a shield, feeling foolish and awkward. How very odd her behavior must appear, creeping in on him this way unannounced.

She took refuge in scolding. "Jared Branden, have you run quite mad? What are you doing out of bed and standing in front of an open window?"

"It's damnably hot in here."

"Is your fever returning?"

"No," he replied irritably. "It's that blasted Frontenac, forever stoking the fire until it's higher than the devil's own flame. I believe he's trying to roast me alive."

Maria started forward, fully intending to shut the window and order Jared back to bed. But he blocked her path, a formidable masculine barrier. She was acutely aware of his musky scent, the way the firelight played over him, turning him into a man of fire and shadow.

He'd lost the haggard look of illness, his profile once again all lean, hard angles. Her gaze traveled from the seductive curve of his mouth, down to the strong cords of his neck, to the intriguing vee of bared chest revealed by the folds of his dressing gown.

Maria tugged at the neckline of her own frock and conceded that for once, Jared was right. It was damnably hot in here.

"I—I suppose it won't hurt to leave the window open," she said. "But only a little."

He grimaced, but moved to comply, lowering the sash until the window only gaped open a crack. The street sounds still filtered in, the rattle of carriages in the square below, a faint lilting of violin music.

"Your neighbors appear to be holding quite a party tonight," he remarked.

"Oh, that must be the Hamiltons. They are forever entertaining. With four unmarried daughters practically on the shelf, I fear they are waxing rather desperate."

"From what I've been hearing, they should stick

with the waltzing and not let any of those girls sing. Not unless their guests have been liberally supplied with champagne."

Maria smiled. "I hope they haven't been disturbing your rest."

"Oh, I've had more than enough rest. I could do with a little disturbing."

"I am not sure you should even be out of bed yet."

"Then you shouldn't have abandoned me to Frontenac these past few days. You could have done a far better job of keeping me between the sheets." His eyes glinted down at her, his voice dropping to a suggestive pitch.

His illness had taken none of the wickedness out of the man, and Maria found herself strangely glad of that. But she replied primly, "I'm sure Frontenac took good care of you, and I have been preoccupied."

"Not with anything regarding the Duke of Sheffield, I hope?"

Maria evaded his piercing gaze. "N-No," she said, and that was not precisely a lie. It didn't have so much to do with Sheffield as the urgent communiqué she had received from Miss Lucas that morning. But Maria refrained from mentioning that. These might well be her last few minutes alone with Jared, and she didn't want to waste them arguing about Miss Lucas.

"I had some shopping to do, a new bonnet to purchase, and—and of course, I have been keeping company with your godmama."

"So I hear," Jared said, folding his arms across his chest. "I gather you ladies have been having some cozy chats over tea. Cheerfully dissecting my character, no doubt. I believe that is what women do to their menfolk when they are not about."

"Actually we were mostly discussing the *children*," Maria said pointedly, and Jared winced. "Your aunt Clarissa is quite interested in our eldest son, where he is going to school. I have been obliged to make up some perfectly deceitful stories about his studies at Harrow."

"Harrow!" Jared frowned. "What the deuce did you tell her we sent him there for? I am an Eton man. I would have made sure my son went to my old school."

"Well, he's my son, too. I could not bear the notion of him being sent so far from our home."

"Damnation, woman. Do you want to keep the boy tied to his mama's leading strings for the—" Jared broke off.

The ridiculousness of their quarrel struck them both at the same time, and her laughter mingled with his. Their eyes met, and Maria felt they shared a certain wistfulness over the sturdy son of their combined imagination, this sweet-faced little boy who had never been.

Jared was quick to look away, and Maria lowered her own eyes.

"I have this odd feeling that your aunt realizes more than we think," Maria said. "I believe she sees through all our nonsense and has been humoring us like a pair of naughty children."

"You may be right. And it's likely just as well. We all have to grow up and stop playing our games of make-believe sooner or later." He spoke lightly, but there was a sadness lurking in his eyes.

Some of her own games of pretend she'd been playing over the years weighed heavily upon Maria. She had never known Jared to be as subdued and thoughtful as he appeared to be tonight. Standing there with him in the silent shadows of her own bedchamber, even the night rhythms of London sounding so far away, she experienced an overwhelming urge to confess to him, tell him things about her past she'd never spoken of before.

But before she could summon up the courage to speak, Jared straightened, seeming to make an effort to shake off his own reflective mood.

"And so what is that you've brought me now?" he asked, indicating the volume she still clutched in her hand. "Some edifying volume of sermons?"

She'd all but forgotten the book, her ostensible excuse for coming to see Jared. "No, not sermons, though I'm sure you could use them."

As she handed him the volume, a slow smile of recognition spread over his face. "Well, what do you know! Old Odysseus returned from the wars."

"You loaned it to me, remember?"

"I remember," he said, his fingers running over the spine in what was almost a caress. "I remember how annoyed you were when I made you read it."

"Odysseus was such a daring hero, but I hated the parts when he seemed weak, falling under the spell of Circe, forgetting all about his faithful Penelope."

"I guess beneath all his heroics, poor Odysseus was just a man, subject to the same temptations and failures as most mortals."

"I'm able to appreciate that a little better now."

Maria entwined her fingers. When she spoke again, her voice was gruff with shyness. "Jared, I—I don't believe I've ever thanked you."

He glanced up from the book, his brows arching with surprise. "For what?"

"For all that you did for me, so long ago. I was a rather ignorant girl. You opened my eyes to so many things, books, music, ideas I'd never dreamed of."

"You're an intelligent woman, Maria. You would have educated yourself in time, or I suppose your husband would have taught you more about the world," Jared said with an almost bitter set to his lips. "Your Count Macaroni must have taken you to all the places we talked about, Athens, Rome, Venice."

Maria squirmed as she always did at Jared's mention of her husband. Once again she was tempted to tell him the truth about Roberto. Instead she said, "We did have a wonderful time traveling until—until—"

"Until the Alp. Yes, I guess that would tend to put a damper on things." Jared's sarcasm did not carry its usual bite. He handed the book back to her. "Here. After all this time, you might as well keep it."

"But it's yours."

"I don't seem to find time for much reading these days."

When she still attempted to protest, he waved the book away with a brusque gesture. "Consider it a belated Valentine's present."

Maria cradled the book in her hands. When she'd been a girl, she dreamed of suitors bringing her exotic flowers, love sonnets, lockets of gold. But she never thought any gesture could have touched her so much as Jared permitting her to keep his book.

"Thank you," she murmured, swallowing a lump in her throat. She set the book down on her dressing table and thought that she should leave.

Besides the extreme impropriety of this late night visit, Jared was looking tired. He lingered by the window, balancing his weight on his good leg, the faint breeze riffling a few dark strands of hair across her brow. Fine lines were etched by his eyes that could have been from fatigue or from something else.

Jared had never been one to parade his emotions, especially not any pain or sadness. He had always been guarded, difficult to reach behind his shield of teasing humor. But in some odd way, he seemed more vulnerable tonight than he had been even when tossing with fever. Maria had never fully understood the man, but she had a strong feeling that if she left him now, she might never have another chance.

She drifted back to his side and stood in silence. There were so many questions she wished to ask him, she hardly knew where to begin. After a moment, she blurted out the first one that came to her head.

"Jared, why did you go into the army?"

Although he looked astonished by the abrupt question, he said, "I think it must have been because of those bright red coats with the shiny buttons—"

"No, really and truly, Jared. Why did you?"

"Really and truly?" he mocked, but he smiled

down at her in a way that was almost tender. "Really and truly, Maria, it's always been the Branden family way since the time of good old Willie the Conqueror."

"But it was never your way."

"No, I guess I'd always dreamed of following a different path."

"What were your dreams, Jared? Do you realize even when we were engaged you never told me?"

He pulled a face. "I'm afraid it was nothing that you'd have found very dashing, Titania."

"I'm older now, and I hope a deal more sensible. Tell me."

He fidgeted with the lace trim on the curtains, looking almost embarrassed. "I used to have these grand literary aspirations, dreaming of becoming another Pope, or Coleridge, or Lamb. A great man of letters. Quite as ridiculous as me fancying I could become a war hero."

"No, it wasn't. You were always so clever, so brilliant, you could have done anything you put your mind to. Why did you give up your dream?"

"Because it was foolish, like the ambitions of so many men when they are young. Most people are not so fortunate to realize their dreams the way you did."

"Me?"

"You went off in search of your knight, your great hero, and you found him, didn't you?"

"I did? Oh! Oh, yes, Roberto," Maria said dully. She was quick to change back to the original subject. "I still don't understand why you went into the army when you'd always been so dead set against it."

"Tradition, my dear, the lure of epic battles, the call of heroism. In the end, it makes fools of all us men." Jared gave a mock sigh. "Though I botched it as usual. Brandens usually don't get themselves maimed. They are supposed to go out in a blaze of glory. But after I'd survived the battle, it seemed decidedly unheroic to succumb to a half-drunk surgeon wielding a hacksaw."

"The doctor who attended you was drunk?" Maria gasped.

"He had a little fondness for gin, but otherwise he was a most amiable fellow. Even if he did keep insisting my leg had to come off. The only way I could persuade him otherwise was a quick game of hazard."

"Hazard!"

"Yes, I tossed him for my leg and won."

It was outrageous and so thoroughly like Jared to have done such a thing when he must have been half out of his mind with pain and the fear of becoming a cripple. Maria knew she ought to laugh, just as she was sure Jared wanted her to do. But she couldn't help it. Her eyes filled with tears.

She tried to duck her head, but it was too late. Jared had seen. He caught her arms, trying to peer into her face. "Here, now, Titania! What's all this? Don't cry. It was just one of my stupid jests."

She tried to blink and smile, but several tears escaped to trail down her cheeks. "I—I can't help it. It—It all sounds so horrid. You—You almost died, and I'm afraid it was my fault."

"Your fault? You fired that cannon at me? I never had any idea. What cracking good aim."

Maria hiccuped on something between a sob and

a chuckle. She dashed her tears away with the back of her hand. "Don't tease, Jared. You know what I mean. I've always been afraid that you wouldn't have gone into the army except for . . . that you only went because I—I—"

"Ah, because you jilted me?"

She nodded glumly, half expecting that he would laugh at her.

Instead he cupped her chin, forcing her to look up, while tucking back a stray tendril that had escaped from the combs holding back her hair. "Poor Titania," he said, but there was more tenderness than mockery in his voice. "Have you been blaming yourself for my folly all this time? Thinking because you would not wed me, I decided to fling my life away, then return to haunt you?"

"Something like that!" she whispered.

"Don't you know I find it much more interesting being able to torment you while I'm still alive?" He ran his hands up her arms in a way that caused her to shiver.

"Much more interesting," he said huskily. "No, Titania. My brief army career was nothing more than an act of youthful stupidity. And I have this leg as a constant reminder."

"Do you mind it so very much?"

"I was bitter for a time right after it happened. But I hardly notice it anymore except . . ."

"Except when?" she prompted when he faltered.

He allowed his hands to slide slowly down her arms, then stepped back from her. "Except at times like the St. Valentine's ball when I have to watch you waltzing with other men."

His words stunned her. "But you hate dancing."

"It could be tolerable . . . with you."

They stared at each other in silence for a moment, the only sounds the crackling of the fire and the faint lilt of music and laughter coming from the house next door.

A mad impulse seized Maria and she caught at Jared's hand. "Let's try it now. Waltz with me."

He looked considerably taken aback. Then he arched one brow. "My dear contessa, you'd best keep your distance. I fear you have taken my fever."

"No, I haven't. I'm quite well." If she was feeling a little overwarm, it had nothing to do with any illness. Trembling a little at the boldness of her own actions, she stepped closer and rested her hand upon Jared's shoulder.

"Please," she whispered.

He stared at her for a moment longer. "Very well," he said. "But if your toes get trampled, don't blame me."

He slipped his arm about her waist, drawing her closer. Maria didn't need the distant throb of the music to help her keep time; her heart seemed to be pounding out the beat for her. They circled her bedchamber slowly, at a pace that had nothing to do with any waltz tempo, but with some rhythm that pulsed between them alone, building and building until Maria felt quite breathless.

"You know why men invented the waltz, don't you?" Jared's dark eyes glinted down at her. "It's just another excuse to get a woman into your arms."

"What makes you think it wasn't a woman's idea?" Maria retorted. Her lashes swept down, and after a brief hesitation, she said almost shyly, "Jared, I have a confession to make."

"Hmmm?" He was holding her so close now, if they had been in a ballroom, every dowager in the place would have fainted from shock.

Maria had to resist an urge to snuggle her head into the strong lee of his shoulder. "At the St. Valentine's Day ball, every man that I waltzed with . . . I kept wishing he was you."

"I have a confession of my own." His voice rumbled so close to her ear, she could feel the warmth of his breath tickle her curls. "I did fix the lottery so you would end up being my valentine."

"Did you? I knew it!" She gave a happy trill of laughter.

"Someone had to save you from my uncle and his corsets."

The front of her bodice brushed against the opening of Jared's dressing gown. She could not help being aware of the lean contours, the heat of the body pulsing beneath that cool satin. She sighed, running her hand caressingly along his shoulder, stroking the nape of his neck.

"I'm awfully glad you don't wear corsets," she murmured. The room seemed to have faded, all but the fire, filling her with a warm glow, making her aware of nothing but Jared's strong arms around her, how perfectly her softer curves seemed to melt against his hard masculinity.

Jared stumbled, which was strange, for they had been barely moving, doing little more than swaying in each other's arms. With a muffled oath, he thrust Maria away from him.

"I can't do this."

"Yes, you can. You were doing fine."

"No, I'm not. I daresay you find this all quite romantic, but there are still a few things you don't understand about real men and women, Titania."

Peering up at him through her own warm haze, Maria saw how flushed he was, a hungry flare in his eyes that made her own warmth turn liquid, molten.

"I understand more now than I used to," she said. "I finally know why you stopped kissing me so much near the end of our courtship. I was so frustrated with you. I had learned to enjoy your kisses, and it seemed like you were holding something back from me, some tantalizing secret."

Reaching up, she traced the outline of his lips with her fingertips. His mouth went taut beneath her touch. Seizing her hand, he stopped her erotic exploration. "Damn it, Maria! What are you trying to do?"

She shook her head slowly, no longer sure herself, confused by the wild feelings that rushed through her veins, longings, regrets, and needs that she had denied until now.

"I remember," she said at last, "the way you used to kiss me. So hot, melting, and sweet. And filled with such promise. I guess I've always wondered where those kisses might have led if—if you hadn't stopped."

She caressed her palms down his chest, stopping just short of grazing against that exposed vee of bared flesh.

"I'm not a green girl anymore, Jared," she whispered.

She felt a shudder course through him, and his hands folded over hers.

"Yes, you are, Maria," he said hoarsely. "You're still searching for things I can never be, looking for things that I can't give."

"Maybe I could learn to value what you can give." Standing on tiptoe, she brushed her mouth against his.

He resisted for but a moment, then he caught her hard against him, kissing her as he never had before, with an intensity that took Maria's breath away.

She knew a brief flicker of fear at the passion she'd unleashed, but it dissolved before her own fire. With a soft whimper, she parted her lips, encouraging his tongue to meld with hers, pressing her body to his, stirring them both to a frenzy of desire.

Jared dragged his mouth from hers. "Maria, please," he rasped. "You're tempting me past bearing. I'm no bloody hero."

"I'm not looking for a hero tonight. Just a man." She cupped his face between her hands. "A not so very ordinary man," she whispered, her eyes misting with desire and tenderness.

To Maria, it seemed it was that look that broke Jared as much as her frantic kisses or her touch. With a low groan, he caught her hard to him, burying his face against her neck.

Sweeping her up in his arms, he carried her over to the bed, unhampered by the awkwardness of his gait. He would have settled her gently upon the mattress, but she entwined her arms about his neck, her eager lips seeking his.

They tumbled as one to the coverlets, Jared shrugging out of his dressing gown. Maria sighed deeply, running her hands over his warm, smooth skin, the solid outline of his muscular chest seeming to glisten in the firelight.

He kissed her again. As his hands moved to undo the lacings of her gown, neither of them noticed when the bedside candle guttered and went out.

Chapter 8

Jared was the first to stir when the morning light peeked past the bed curtains. He opened his eyes slowly, half fearing that he would find Maria gone, along with the mists of sleep.

But he rolled over and she was still there, nestled at his side. Scarce daring to breathe, he propped up on one elbow to stare down at her, amazed by the depth of feeling that rushed through him at the sight of her, sleeping so peacefully. She looked almost ephemeral, like the faerie queen he delighted in calling her. Her nose had a proud tilt to it even in slumber, and her blond hair tumbled like sunlight across the pillow, her gold-tipped lashes fanning against the delicate pallor of her cheeks. Her breasts rose and fell in a soft rhythm, the coral tips barely concealed by the ivory counterpane.

She'd done a fair job of pirating most of the covers, Jared noted with tender amusement. He could feel the drafts of chill morning air against his bare backside. But he made no effort to reclaim Maria's booty from her. Rather he eased the sheets up higher over her creamy shoulder and gently brushed back a golden curl that had tumbled across her eyes.

Images crowded into his mind of all that had passed between them last night, once more arousing his desire, leaving him rather shaken, awestruck as well.

It had been like . . . like the wedding night they'd never had. He'd never imagined he was capable of loving any woman like that, with such tenderness, losing himself completely in another's desires. And Maria, so shy, but responding with a passion that had overcome any modesty, her eagerness fast hurling them both to a state of mutual bliss.

When they had joined together, it had been as though nothing had ever come between them, not a broken engagement, or a Valentine's Day lost, or even an Italian nobleman with a preposterous name and title.

But Jared frowned, for he knew that wasn't true. That was what confused him. A great deal had come between them over the past ten years, not the least of which was Maria's marriage. She was no longer the innocent girl he'd once known. She had been very much a woman in his arms last night, and yet . . .

Suspicions about Maria crowded his mind that were almost a dead certainty. But it was a certainty that made no sense.

He tried to forget these troubling doubts, settle back beside her. But the urge to touch her, to draw her back into his arms, the need to have her respond to him as she'd done last night, was far too strong.

Bending over her, he proceeded to kiss her slowly

and thoroughly awake. Just like in the faerie tales Maria so loved, Jared thought, suppressing a smile.

She wriggled beneath him, her eyes still closed. Her tongue moistened her mouth as though savoring his kiss in a manner that sent a shaft of desire piercing through him. Her lashes drifted open and she regarded him sleepily, her lips curving in languorous fashion.

Then her eyes widened with alarm. As she came fully awake, she gasped and started to emit a piercing shriek. Startled himself by this unexpected reaction to his kiss, Jared barely managed to muffle her outcry with his hand.

"Shh! Maria. It's all right. It's me. Don't you re— Ow!" He wrenched his hand away when she bit him.

Looking frightened and disoriented, she scrambled to the far corner of the bed, dragging the coverlets with her. So much for faerie-tale endings, Jared thought, nursing his injured thumb.

"J-Jared," she stammered, staring at him wildly. "What—What are you doing in my bed? And you're naked!"

"So are you. And you've got all the covers," he said irritably. For once in his life, he'd been feeling as though he might have been able to spout some of that tender romantic nonsense to Maria, but the mood was sadly shattered as he had to struggle for one corner of the sheet to maintain his own dignity.

She had the counterpane dragged up to the level of her eyes, and she peered at him across the satiny surface. "Then I wasn't dreaming. You—I—we—we really did . . ."

"Yes, I'm afraid we did." He gave a bitter sigh.

"Just as I was afraid you would be heartily sorry for it in the morning."

"Oh, no!"

His disgruntled remark at least had the effect of drawing her partly from beneath the covers. She lowered the counterpane to the level of her neck and gave him a shy smile. "I'm not in the least sorry. I—I was just a little overcome, remembering. It was all beyond anything I'd ever imagined. Thank you, Jared. You have no idea how much I—I appreciated everything."

Jared felt his own discomfiture evaporate. He wanted to laugh. He wanted to cover her face with kisses, but she looked so serious, he forced himself to reply gravely, "You're very welcome, Contessa. Would you like to shake my hand in congratulations?"

"Congratulations for what?"

As he arched his brows in wicked fashion and she took his meaning, she gasped, "You horrid, arrogant man."

Her earnestness dissolved into giggles and she hit him with her pillow. In the process of fending her off, she somehow ended up in Jared's arms. He claimed her lips in the sort of early morning kiss he had envisioned, long, slow, and sweet. But as she rested her head against his shoulder with a contented sigh, he noticed she was still taking care to keep as much of the coverlet as possible trapped between their naked flesh.

There was an air of modesty, of shyness, about Maria in the light of day that Jared sensed could be easily coaxed away. But its very existence only strengthened the suspicions he'd harbored about last night.

Perhaps he should let it go. He had no right prying into any of Maria's secrets, but he couldn't seem to help himself either. Tangling his hand in the silken strands of her hair, he sought for some delicate way to voice his question, but there didn't seem to be any.

Pressing his lips close to her ear, he murmured, "Maria, why didn't you tell me you were still a virgin?"

He felt her tense immediately, although she said, "I'm not. I mean I—I wasn't. How absurd. I was married for six years. I'm—I'm the Contessa di Montifiori Vincerone."

"I know. The widow of a man who had trouble keeping his balance on mountain paths." Jared couldn't help wondering what else the noble Count Roberto had had trouble with.

"Maria, you don't have to pretend with me," he said. "I've had enough experience with women."

"Seduced a good many virgins, have you?"

"No, only one. And that was last night."

Maria's lips pursed into a frown. "Is this your way of saying you found me clumsy and inexperienced?"

"No, I found you wonderful. But I can't help suspecting this was the first time you ever had a man in your bed. Was it?" he prodded gently.

Maria wriggled away from him, avoiding his eyes. "Goodness, look at the time. Your valet could come in on us at any minute."

"Frontenac has more regard for his life than to disturb me at this hour. Maria . . ."

He sensed her instinct to bolt from the bed, and forestalled it. Levering himself up onto one elbow, Jared trapped her beneath the weight of his arm. She tried to distract him by nibbling kisses along the line of his jaw.

It almost worked, but Jared took a fortifying breath and pinned her firmly to the mattress. "Maria, you didn't answer my question."

"I forget what it was." She angled a sultry glance up at him through the thickness of her lashes. But when she realized such tactics were not going to work with him, her mouth formed in a soft pout.

She squirmed beneath his touch, her face turning a bright pink. After a moment more of resistance, she sighed and said, "All right. Maybe I was still a virgin."

"Maybe!"

"All right! I—I was."

He released her, her answer just what he'd expected. Why, then, did he still feel a little stunned to hear her admit it? As he sank back against the mattress, Maria rose up, regarding him anxiously.

"It doesn't make any difference, does it?"

"No," he said slowly. "Only in that I would have been more gentle with you."

"You could not have been any more gentle than you were." She caressed her hand lightly over the bared plane of his chest, nuzzling her head against his shoulder. Her touch, the soft look in her eyes, was a clear invitation, but Jared did not respond. He never thought he'd see the time when he would want to talk more than engage in other activities in bed. But damn it! The woman could not just fling out such a puzzling confession, then expect him to think no more about it.

For the last ten years of his life, he had believed that Maria had belonged body and soul to another man. It appeared he had been at least half-wrong.

She curled her fingers in the dark whorls of hair that matted his chest. He seized her hand to still the distracting gesture. "Maria, I realize your past is none of my concern. I have no right to ask any more questions. But I simply don't understand how—I mean why—why your marriage was never consummated."

"Well, Roberto and I were always so busy, we never seemed to get around to—"

"Maria!"

She flinched at the reproof in his voice, and he added more gently, "There is no reason for you to be embarrassed about telling me the truth. Whatever the problem was in your marriage, I'm sure it was no fault of yours."

Jared hated himself for prying this way, seeking out memories that must be distressful to Maria. She moved away from him and sat up. But to his surprise, her lips curved in a rather impish smile.

"Yes, the problem definitely was Roberto," she said. "You see . . . I—I made him up."

"You what?" Jared jerked bolt upright.

"I invented him. The whole thing, his looks, his name, his title. The grand Conte Roberto di Montifiori Vincerone. A complete and utter fraud."

"But—But the portrait!"

"I painted it myself from my memories—I mean out of my own imagination."

"And your fortune?"

"Oh, I inherited that from my aunt."

Jared could only stare at her. "You mean to tell me this noble husband of yours was nothing more than—than a fantasy, another one of your faerie stories?"

Maria gave an apologetic shrug. "Yes, I fear he was."

Jared sank back so sharply, he cracked his head against the bedpost. But he scarce noticed the pain, his mind reeling from what she'd just told him more than any physical blow. He could hardly believe it. Of all the things he might have guessed about Maria's marriage, this was one that would never have occurred to him. That it hadn't been real, Maria's beloved Roberto had never existed.

Pressing his hand to his brow, Jared said, "Maria, I think you'd better explain this to me, slowly, in a way that even a dolt like me can understand."

She plumped up the pillows and settled them more snugly behind her back. "There isn't much to explain. After our broken engagement, my papa was so disappointed, he wanted me gone— That is, he was dreadfully concerned about me. So he sent me to live with my mother's older sister who was a widow, my aunt Harriet.

"She was this remarkable, eccentric old woman. I grew to be very fond of her, and she of me. You would have liked her. She always wore red garters."

"Red garters," Jared muttered. "What does this have to do with the Count Macaroni?"

"I'm getting to that. Be patient. You see, Aunt Harriet thought England terribly damp and uncultured. She preferred traveling abroad, and so she swept me off to Italy. She wasn't even deterred by the fact that Napoleon had invaded. Once a contingent of the French army was only two miles from—"

"Maria!" Jared interrupted this flow of reminiscences. "The count?"

"Oh, yes. Roberto. He did not come into being until . . ." Maria's smile faded. "Until my aunt lay dying. It quite diverted her in her last hours, helping to invent a husband for me."

"But in the devil's name, why, Maria? Why invent a husband when—" Jared stopped himself just short of adding, when she had left a real one waiting on the church doorstep.

Maria plucked at the coverlet as she said in a small voice, "Inventing Roberto was Aunt Harriet's notion to protect both me and the fortune she left. You cannot know what it is like for a young, unwed female. You have no freedom, no control over your own destiny. But as a married lady, the wealthy contessa, I was able to do just as I liked, and who would say me nay? Certainly not Roberto."

"Oh, certainly not. Especially since you'd already dropped him off a convenient Alp."

Maria laughed at Jared's tart remark, but he felt no temptation to join her. He supposed he should have been amused by her confession. It beat the deception that he had practiced upon his aunt Clarissa all hollow, made Jared seem a rank amateur by comparison. Maria had managed to hoax the entire ton, including himself.

But far from being amused, Jared was beset by a sharp feeling of betrayal. It was a hard thing to admit, but he had been jealous of her Count Roberto, jealous of a figment of Maria's imagination. Damn it all, he feared that he still was bitterly envious, hurt by the fact Maria had preferred even a make-believe man over the prospect of being Mrs. Jared Branden.

Shifting slightly on the pillows, Maria laid her hand lightly on his arm. "Well, so now you know my deep, dark secret. I trust my little deception will be safe with you, Branden."

"As safe as such a cork-brained secret could ever be," he remarked irritably.

"I've managed to carry it off for over five years now. No one has ever guessed. Not even you."

"There were moments when I suspected there was something deuced odd about your count."

"No, you didn't. You even believed the story about the Alp."

So he had. That's partly what was so annoying. Maria had managed to make a complete cake of him. It didn't help Jared's temper to perceive a faint trace of smugness in her. He had to curb a strong urge to shake her.

When she tried to nestle back against him, he folded his arms across his chest in a forbidding fashion. "It's a pity you didn't choose to confide this to me last night."

"Last night," she murmured. "It didn't seem all that important."

"Not important!" He glared at her. "You must have a poor notion of my honor."

"Your honor?" She blinked at him as though he had run mad. "What does your honor have to do with this?"

"Only this. I don't bed unmarried females."

"But it was perfectly all right when you thought I was a widow?"

"Not perfectly all right, but—but different," he sputtered, annoyed because she dared to make it sound as though he were the illogical one. "The point is, you're not a widow. You're not even the Contessa Macaroni. You're still Maria Addams, a foolish daydreaming little—"

He broke off, flinging up his hands in exasperation. "Well, there's no help for it this time. We will have to be married."

"What?" She shrank back as though he'd boxed her ears.

"It is not my habit to ruin females."

Maria's cheeks flushed with indignation. "Who says I'm ruined?"

"You were a virgin. And I—"

"In the eyes of the world, I am still a respectable widow. I am entitled to have my amours as long as I'm discreet. No one knows any different."

"But I know, damn it," Jared snapped. "You will have to wed me, Maria. There is no use arguing about it."

"This is about as charming as the first proposal you ever made me."

"I don't recall it."

"That's because you never made one!" She smacked her fist against the mattress, expelling her breath in a huff. "You simply told me you were going to marry me, the way you are now. My answer is still the same. No!"

She scrambled out of bed, her breasts heaving with indignation, affording Jared a tantalizing glimpse of all the charms he'd sampled last night.

She snatched up the first garment she found, Jared's dressing gown, and began struggling into it.

That left Jared with little choice as he bolted after her. Wrenching the bed sheet with him, he draped it over himself toga fashion.

"This is not settled by a long shot, Maria," he raged. "Where do you think you're going?"

"Back to the guest room before I am 'ruined,' as you so sweetly put it. My maid must already have noticed my absence. I have no desire to announce it to the rest of the household."

"That's exactly what's going to happen if you oblige me to pursue you down the hall wearing a bed sheet."

"Where's your dressing gown? Oh." Maria stole a glance downward as though realizing for the first time what she wore. She hugged the wine-colored folds closer to herself. "Well, feel free to borrow anything of mine."

She made an effort to bolt past him, but Jared leaned up against the door, barring her way. "Maria, we have to talk."

"We can talk later over tea."

"You want to discuss your lost virginity over toast and crumpets?"

"I don't want to discuss it at all." She stamped her bare foot against the carpet. "Or your infamous proposal."

"Infamous proposal?" Jared rolled his eyes. He was attempting to salvage this situation, and she was behaving as if he'd insulted her. "This may come as quite a shock to you, Maria. But some people don't just go around pretending to be married.

They really do it. You might look to your own parents for example."

For some reason the mention of her parents had a curious effect on Maria. She paled a little. "You—You leave my parents out of this. I am not like my mother. I—I am not interested in marriage."

"Still waiting for your knight in shining armor, I suppose?" Jared sneered.

"No," she replied in a small voice.

"After last night, are you going to deny the attraction that exists between us?"

"We've always been attracted. It just doesn't seem to be enough, Jared."

Jared paced off a few steps, raking his hand back through his hair in pure frustration. "Then what the deuce do you propose we do? Pretend that last night never happened?"

Maria shook her head, then suggested hesitantly, "We—We could become lovers."

"Lovers!" Jared almost choked on the word.

Maria raised her chin in a defensive posture. "It is a very fashionable practice amongst the ton, or so I'm told. Even romantic. Just think of the story of Lady Hamilton and Lord Nelson."

"I have no desire to be like Lord Nelson. He had vital parts shot off him." Jared realized he sounded as sulky and unreasonable as a thwarted schoolboy. It only added to his sense of annoyance.

Maria's lashes swept down. She no longer appeared angry so much as saddened. "Perhaps it would be better for both of us to discuss this at some distant date when we are both calmer. I may have to leave London for a while, but when I get back—"

"Leave?" Jared demanded. "Where are you going?"

The way she avoided meeting his gaze was answer enough. Jared swore. "It's that Lucas chit again, isn't it?"

Maria nodded.

Jared expelled an exasperated breath. Here he was making a fool of himself, trying to declare himself to Maria while wrapped up in a bed sheet, and all along she was thinking about that silly Lucas girl.

"Miss Lucas is in great distress," Maria said. "Her marriage is scheduled to take place sooner than either of us suspected. I received a frantic letter from her yesterday through the milliner that we both patronize."

"The milliner!" Jared muttered. "Of course. That's why you made so many blasted trips to that shop since you returned to London."

Maria regarded him with suspicion and surprise. "You were spying on me?"

"No, I paid someone else to do it."

His blunt admission left Maria looking rather nonplussed. He was almost afraid she would ask him why he'd done such a thing, and he didn't have any good answer.

To his relief, she merely angled a curious glance at him, then continued. "I don't see any chance of rescuing Miss Lucas in town, but I have been thinking of a plan to intercept her coach and . . . and you probably think I'm mad."

"Not probably," Jared said.

"There is just no way to explain to you why helping Miss Lucas is so important to me." Maria hung her head and added, "There is no way to make you understand."

She was right about that. Jared only understood one thing. Maria was rejecting him again, and it cut as deeply as it ever had. This time when she moved to slip quietly out the bedroom door, he made no move to stop her.

Let her go, Jared thought bitterly. Off to play heroine or guardian angel or whatever role she was fantasizing herself in this time. It was obvious he and Maria had nothing left to discuss, now or at any other time.

Become lovers? He could hardly believe she'd suggested such a thing. Such a sophisticated arrangement might have worked with dozens of other noble ladies of the ton, but not Maria. Because she was still as naive as a schoolroom miss. Because she was still a romantic, a starry-eyed dreamer.

And because . . . he loved her. Perhaps more now than he ever had. After last night, the realization was not as staggering to him as it once might have been. His demand that she marry him had nothing to do with her lost virginity and his honor. It had everything to do with the fact that he loved her.

He could at least admit that to himself, if not to her. But Maria ought to be able to tell, damn it. She knew that he had never been one to spout pretty phrases. Hellfire, in his family, it had been a sign of affection to salute.

Jared sagged down on the edge of the bed. So now what? Strange, but he was no longer as cynical as he had been in his youth, able to shrug off being left by Maria at the church door. Perhaps because he knew a little more of life now, the emptiness, the loneliness, it could bring. He needed Maria. He loved her. And he fancied she was not entirely indifferent to him either.

But what the devil was it going to take to win that stubborn woman? An idea filtered into his mind, one that he entertained with so little welcome, he cringed at the thought of it.

He was still stewing over the alarming notion when Frontenac entered the bedchamber some time later. The valet's brows rose in mild astonishment to find Jared perched on the edge of the bed, attired in a sheet, his chin propped on his hand like a pose of some ancient Roman statue.

Jared forestalled any impudent remark by asking, "The clothes I was wearing the night I took ill. What did you do with the mask?"

Frontenac sniffed, his gaze drifting over Jared. "I believe monsieur stands in need of a little more apparel than a mask."

"Don't be an idiot, man. Did you save the mask or didn't you?"

"I would never throw any of monsieur's belongings away without asking first." Frontenac drew himself up, looking offended. But curiosity won out over his ruffled feelings. "Does monsieur mean to attend another masquerade?"

"No," Jared answered in abstracted fashion, "I'm planning to go tilt at windmills."

If Jared derived no other satisfaction from that morning, at least he knew the pleasure of watching Frontenac's mouth drop open.

Chapter 9

Lurking beneath the shadows of the trees, Jared kept a firm rein on his restive mount. He peered through the slits of his mask towards the ribbon of road illuminated by moonlight. Staines Road, one of the most notorious byways leading through Hounslow Heath, the site where many an infamous highwayman had plied his trade. Most of those bold rogues were gone now, ridden off into legend or having met their doom by the hangman's noose. But the aura of danger, of mystery, they had left behind seemed to linger.

A chill wind ruffled the ends of Jared's cloak as he studied that dark and silent roadway. His heartbeat quickening, he experienced many of the same sensations as he had on the plains of the Spanish Peninsula when he had faced the French army, the same thought chasing through his brain.

What the hell am I doing here?

Since he had no satisfactory answer to that question, he wheeled his horse about and rode towards where his two companions awaited him, their horses concealed deeper within the shelter of Staines Wood.

They were an odd assortment for a band of ruthless brigands, Jared thought, quirking his lips as he caught sight of Frontenac, tangled in his own cape. His mask had slipped again, falling partly over his eyes. As Frontenac struggled to right it, still clutching a pistol in his other hand, it was a question of what the skinny valet was most likely to do first, fall off his horse or accidentally shoot himself.

Then there was Maria, her golden hair and face obscured beneath a floppy-brimmed hat sporting a pink feather. The pair of breeches she wore clung to her curves in a way that was likely to fool no one into thinking she was a man, unless the moon was gracious enough to duck behind some clouds.

Not for the first time, Jared reflected, he might have a better chance of bringing this nonsense off without his fellow conspirators. But in the event something went wrong, he could think of no other servant or friend he could have trusted besides Frontenac. For all his irritating mannerisms, the valet was unfailingly discreet. If Jared did make an idiot of himself tonight, he would have to hear about it from Frontenac for the rest of his life, but at least the tale would not be spread all over London.

As for Maria . . . Jared frowned. He would as soon have kept her out of the risky part of this business, but there had been no possibility of that. It still piqued him when he remembered her reaction to his volunteering his services, the doubtful expression that had crossed her face.

She might have been a little more impressed.

True, he supposed he could have framed his offer a little more graciously than "All right. I'll go rescue the damned chit."

But Maria needn't have acted as though she hardly trusted him to bring the thing off, as though he would forget all about Miss Lucas the minute Maria's back was turned. Though truth to tell— Jared grimaced—more than once during this past week of preparations for tonight, he had been tempted to do so. He still had a strong urge to wheel his horse around and . . .

"Ah, well." He shrugged, his mouth twisting into a self-mocking grimace as he muttered, "No time to be having an attack of good sense now, Don Quixote. This appears to be the night you prove your mettle to the lady."

As Jared drew his horse cautiously alongside hers, Maria peered at him from beneath her hat brim. She asked in an anxious voice, "Any sign of the carriage yet?"

"Nothing."

Frontenac sniffed. "It would be better if we all waited and watched closer to the road."

"After the way you went haring off the last time," Jared growled, "not on your life."

Maria sprang to Frontenac's defense. "It was an honest mistake. In the dark, all these carriages look alike."

Jared glowered at her. "It wasn't you who had to apologize for waylaying the wrong coach. I felt a perfect fool."

"But the lady was very gracious," Frontenac pointed out. "She was willing to give monsieur her purse anyway, if you had been so kind as to accept it."

"Frontenac, there is a larcenous side to your nature I never suspected before."

"I was never called upon to play the part of the highwayman before, monsieur."

"We are not highwaymen. We're knights errant. Think of yourself as my Sancho Panza."

Frontenac apparently found the notion quite revolting, for he nudged his mount and drew apart from Jared and Maria. "I shall take up my station closer to the road, monsieur. Someone needs to be keeping better watch."

Jared did not rebuke him this time, but let him go. Rolling his eyes, he remarked to Maria, "Now I've offended him. I keep forgetting. Frontenac has dignity. I don't."

"You shouldn't tease the poor man so. He's excessively loyal to you," Maria said. "And if you mean to start complaining about our mission—"

"Heaven forfend," Jared cut her off hastily. "I live but to serve you, milady. Have I said one disparaging word?"

Maria was obliged to admit that he hadn't. That was the thing she found almost as puzzling as Jared's presence here at all tonight. After she had rejected him again, she had been despairingly certain that it must at last be the end of everything between her and Jared. Then he had stunned her by marching into her parlor that same afternoon and announcing, after his usual offhand fashion, that he would help her rescue Miss Lucas after all.

She had no idea what had caused him to change

his mind. Maria wondered if she ever would understand the enigmatic man that was Jared Branden.

His gloved hand looped lightly about the reins, he yet managed to keep an iron control over his spirited black gelding. Jared claimed his leg kept him from riding with the same dash he once had, but Maria had seen no sign of that tonight. He still sat a horse far better than she.

As though growing impatient of the waiting, Jared wrenched off his mask. Moonlight filtering through the trees illuminated the hard cast of his profile, but his expression was still unreadable.

Maria found herself studying him and recollecting many of the things that Jared's aunt Clarissa had told her about "these Branden men."

It takes a deal of persistence to find the love and tenderness ... kept hidden beneath the tarnished armor. And yet, despite the lack of pretty words, he is there when you need him most.

Maria sighed. Perhaps in the past she had given up on Jared far too easily. She might never hear him admit why he had come with her tonight, that despite his cynical facade, he was a man capable of great caring.

She could only be sure of one thing. That she loved him and that, reluctant hero or not, he was here. Perhaps that was all that really mattered.

As though becoming aware of her scrutiny, Jared fidgeted with the reins and broke the silence that seemed to press in upon them, disturbed only by the rustling of the trees, the whickering of the horses. Jared remarked, "It would have been so much easier if that silly Lucas girl would have found a way to slip out of her uncle's house and come to us in London."

"I suppose it would have," Maria agreed. She wasn't about to explain that Miss Lucas was incapable of taking any such vigorous action on her own behalf. If Jared had any notion of how languishing and weepy Selina Lucas really was, Maria feared he would bolt all the way back to town.

Jared adjusted the folds of his multicaped cloak. "Well, at least it is not as cold as the last time I followed you on your moonlight escapades, Titania."

"I trust you won't take a chill again," Maria said anxiously.

"It might be worth it to be cured so charmingly in your bed."

It was the first time either of them had made any reference to what had happened between them during Jared's sojourn beneath her roof. Suddenly, far from being cold, the night seemed to pulse with heated memories. She sensed that Jared felt it, too, for he squirmed in the saddle and looked away.

"Perhaps we had better review the plan," he said abruptly.

"Again?" Maria groaned.

"It appears to be necessary after the fiasco with the last coach. I swear Frontenac had his pistol trained on my back instead of on the coachman. And you just sat there, making no move to go to the coach door."

"You were already there ahead of me."

"What was I supposed to do when that female opened the door and started to faint?"

"It was very convenient how she timed her swoon until you were able to catch her."

"All things considered, I thought the young lady very brave."

"And extremely well endowed," Maria said tartly.

Jared scowled. "Are we here to argue or rescue Miss Lucas? The plan, Maria?"

Maria gave a long-suffering sigh. "Frontenac is to cover the coachman. You will take care of any postilions. I am to go to the door and fetch Miss Lucas out and spirit her off into the woods, where you and Frontenac will join me."

"Then we all ride like the devil towards Hounslow and hope to God the coach I hired is ready and waiting." Jared added dourly, "I also hope to hell that we have no Sheffield to deal with."

"Miss Lucas clearly stated in her last message that the duke would not be traveling with her in the coach. I expect only her maid or her chaperon."

"So you keep telling me, but I find that deuced odd."

"What do you mean?"

"Sheffield's been so careful with the girl up until now. Knowing His Grace, one would have thought he would have sent his niece off with at least a dozen outriders."

"Miss Lucas says that her fiancé, Sir Arthur, prefers simplicity. He abhors anything that smacks of pomp and circumstance. And Sheffield would hardly like to make it seem as if the bride was meeting her intended under armed guard."

"That may be so, but we'd best be prepared in any case." Beneath the edge of Jared's cloak, Maria caught the metallic gleam of his pistol.

She shuddered. "Y-e-es. But I don't actually want to shoot anybody."

"Nor do I," Jared said. "I don't mind being hanged for abduction, but I draw the line at murder."

"No one will be hanged. When we get Miss Lucas safe away, we will publish her wrongs to the world, and Sheffield will no longer dare to persecute her. And I daresay Sir Arthur won't want to marry her anymore when he discovers she's not willing."

"I can't imagine why he'd want to marry her even if she was," Jared muttered.

"Miss Lucas is a perfectly lovely girl even if she is a bit . . ."

"Hen-witted?"

Maria frowned at him. "When this is all over, I am sure I can match Miss Lucas up with some nice young man."

"And we'll all live happily ever after," Jared drawled, but he didn't appear terribly convinced of that fact.

Maria was not sure that she was. Oh, she had no qualms for Miss Lucas. It was herself and Jared that she wondered about. She had told herself that she would be contented enough by the fact that Jared had come with her tonight. That she would not press him for his reasons. But she did not seem able to help herself.

After another awkward pause, she asked, "Jared, what made you change your mind? Why did you decide to join me in helping Miss Lucas?"

He shrugged, seeming to take great care to shift in the saddle so that his face was cast into shadow by the rustling branches of the trees. "Why, to save the idiotic girl from a fate worse than death.

Though I always wondered if whoever coined that phrase had actually ever tried dying."

"Have you grown so fond of Miss Lucas then?"

Jared snorted. "After tonight, if anyone ever mentions that chit's name to me again, I'll throw myself off an Alp."

"Then why?" Maria persisted.

"It's just the usual stupid—I mean noble sort of thing we lunatics in shining armor do."

"You've never believed in any of that nonsense before. Why are you playing at knighthood now?"

In spite of the concealing darkness, she saw him compress his lips.

"You know bloody well why!" he exploded at last.

He urged his horse close enough so that he could lean out of the saddle. He caught Maria by the nape of the neck. Nearly dislodging her hat, he hauled her forward and planted a long, hard kiss on her mouth.

The pent-up feelings that Jared had suppressed for the past week surged through his veins, and he all but wrenched her out of the saddle. He'd tried to act the hero, chivalrous, disinterested, expecting no reward, but he'd had about all of this nobility bilge that he could stand.

When he released her, Maria was gasping for breath and clutching at the reins to maintain her balance. His own pulse thundering, Jared was on the verge of dismounting to tug her down into his arms, forgetting everything but—

"*Alors*, monsieur!"

Frontenac's cry cut through the night, reminding Jared that he and Maria were not alone, reminding him also of what they were out here for.

He let fly a soft curse.

"*À moi*, monsieur. The coach. It comes."

"Alert the whole countryside while you're at it," Jared grumbled. He turned regretfully to Maria, but she was already responding to Frontenac's call.

As her horse surged past him, Jared had no choice but to follow. He caught up to her just as she emerged from the trees to join Frontenac by the roadside.

The excited valet indicated the blink of running lights in the distance, the faint clatter of horses' hooves now audible as well.

"This has to be the one, monsieur."

"I hope so. If we have to stop every coach that passes, we'll be here all damned night."

"This is the right one. I feel it in my bones, monsieur. But if it isn't and this time a lady should chance to offer her purse again—"

"Frontenac!" Jared had a feeling his prim valet was never going to be the same again after this night.

As the carriage rattled closer, Jared tried to issue calm directions, but to no avail. Frontenac galloped out from the trees, brandishing his pistol like a madman.

In his excitement, he forgot himself and issued his command to halt in French. For a moment, Jared feared the coach and four would thunder right over Frontenac. But the coachman appeared to understand the significance of the mask and pistol, for he sawed back on the reins, drawing the carriage to a halt.

Jared felt the situation slipping rapidly out of his control as Maria eagerly charged forward, not waiting for Jared to cover her. With a curse, Jared urged his own mount into the roadway, then realized he had forgotten to replace his mask. As if it would make a difference, he thought with a shrug. Sheffield would have to be a complete dolt not to figure out who was responsible for this night's work.

The coachman, his hands already held high, cried out, "Don't shoot." The portly man appeared astonished and shaky, but not more so than the pistol in Frontenac's hands. Jared groaned when Maria again rode in front of him.

Jared started to draw out his own pistol when a horse and rider thundered out of nowhere. Jared caught a brief flash of black cloak, a sinister eye patch. Sheffield. Bearing down on Maria, waving his sword. With a cry of warning, Jared drove his mount in between them.

Sheffield's horse shied back. He slashed wildly at Jared. Jared cursed, feeling the sword's point bite into his thigh. He leapt, knocking the duke out of the saddle.

They both fell heavily, the weapon flying from Sheffield's hand. As they hit the ground, Jared grappled with the duke. He pinned Sheffield on his back, bringing his own pistol to bear.

His Grace's wig toppled off, the gleam of his bald pate in the moonlight nothing to the glare in his eye.

"Branden," he grunted. "Have—you run mad?"

Jared was too winded to assure His Grace that yes indeed, he had. He raised his head enough to confront a circle of wide eyes. The coachman,

Frontenac, even Maria, had dismounted and stood gaping in horror.

Jared jerked his head impatiently towards the coach door.

Maria stared blankly, not comprehending.

"Miss Lucas," Jared reminded her in a furious hiss.

Seeming to snap out of her trance, Maria made haste towards the coach door.

Jared caught a movement at the rear of the coach, the stealthy creeping of a footman. "Don't try anything," Jared barked. "If you value your master's life."

Jared doubted that any of them did. He hoped they at least had some respect for the source of their wages.

Sheffield attempted to pull free. Jared waved the pistol in his face, and he subsided.

"I'll see you in hell for this," the duke sputtered.

"Too late. I've already been there."

While Sheffield fumed in a helpless rage, Jared became acutely conscious of the searing pain in his thigh, blood seeping through the fabric of his breeches.

Maria seemed to be taking an eternity about hauling Miss Lucas from the coach. Holding open the door, Maria leaned inside the carriage. Jared could hear her expostulating with someone in the depths of the coach, but he could not make out the words.

What the devil was amiss? Had that stupid Lucas girl lost her nerve or swooned? Jared ground his teeth at the prospect. If he had to, he'd yank her out himself by the hair.

When Maria retreated from the carriage, alone, a sinking feeling settled in the pit of Jared's stomach. His foreboding only increased as Maria approached him. It was obvious she was having great difficulty meeting his eye.

"Well, where is the girl?" he demanded, taking great care not to allow the pistol to waver from Sheffield for a second. "Don't tell me. The girl's not there. This was all some sort of clever ruse, devised by His Grace."

From the smirk that crossed Sheffield's features, Jared was almost ready to believe it.

But Maria made haste to say, "Oh, no, Miss Lucas is in the coach." She paused, fretting her lip. "And so is Sir Arthur. He—He came to fetch his bride after all."

"Is he holding her prisoner? Go threaten him with your pistol."

"Sir Arthur isn't holding her, at least not in any fashion that Miss Lucas dislikes. Apparently he—he shaved off his beard. He looks rather handsome."

Jared scowled at Maria. "What the devil has that got to say to anything?"

"Everything. It—It seems Miss Lucas fell in love with Sir Arthur at first sight." Maria gulped, then added in a small voice, "She does not desire to be rescued anymore."

"She doesn't what?" Jared rasped as the full import of Maria's words sank in. He'd made a complete ass of himself playing highwayman, his favorite riding cloak was torn and disheveled, his pant leg was soaked with blood, he had one of the most vindictive peers in England sprawled beneath him in the dirt.

And Miss Lucas did not desire to be rescued anymore!

Lowering his pistol, Jared let fly a string of oaths that caused even Sheffield to blanch.

Chapter 10

The merest scratch—that was the pronounce-
ment of the physician who looked after Jared's
wound. Dr. Marsden, a round little man with twin-
kling eyes, appeared not in the least disconcerted
to be summoned to a Hounslow inn at this hour of
night to attend a gentleman suffering from a sword
wound.

In his present surly humor, Jared thought he
preferred his physicians drunk to one so briskly
cheerful. If Marsden told him one more time how
fortunate he was to only have been grazed, Jared
was going to graze him with the poker iron.

But at least the doctor had had the decency to
chase Maria out of the room while he had cleaned
up Jared's wound. It had been a great relief to
Jared. He'd been able to stop heroically clenching
his teeth and instead swear fluently while Dr.
Marsden took a few quick stitches to close the gash.

After the good doctor took his leave, Jared shifted the bed sheet to survey the damage for himself.
His leg had stopped bleeding and was tightly ban-
daged. But any movement was painful. Why did it
have to be the same damn leg as the last time he'd
been injured?

Jared was cursing softly when his valet entered. The events of the evening appeared to have sobered Frontenac considerably, cured him of his brief fascination with the life of a highwayman. It seemed that the valet sickened at the sight of blood. At any other time, the discovery of such a failing in the indomitable Frontenac might have cheered Jared considerably, but he was in no humor to find anything amusing at present.

The little Frenchman still looked pale as he inquired, "All is well with you, monsieur?"

"I'm no longer spouting blood like an overfed leech, if that's what you mean."

"Monsieur . . . I beg you." Frontenac clutched his stomach in an expressive gesture.

"You shouldn't be up here attending me anyway," Jared growled. "I told you to keep an eye on the contessa."

"Milady is belowstairs in the kitchen, taking tea and having a long chat with the landlady of this establishment."

"Oh God!" Jared struggled frantically to a sitting position. "Maria's probably wheedling out the woman's entire life story. Next we'll be rescuing her from persecution."

"Oh, no, the landlady appears too large and redoubtable a female to be persecuted. Monsieur must not agitate himself."

Jared subsided with a deep sigh. He'd been astonished they had even been permitted to cross the threshold of a respectable establishment like the White Hart. They'd been a most disreputable-looking trio, Jared dripping blood on the taproom floor, Maria scandalously clad in breeches,

Frontenac's mask falling from his pocket at the most inopportune moment. The host had eyed them askance, but Maria had taken charge, storming the man's defenses with her flashing blue eyes. The woman certainly knew how to play the countess when she had to. In short order, she had not only secured Jared the best bedchamber, but also had a doctor fetched as well.

Jared didn't even know what purpose he had served on this little venture, besides providing the comic relief. An image assailed him of that grim moment back on the road when he had been obliged to let Sheffield up off the ground and tender a gruff apology.

What would Dox Quixote have done in such a situation, Jared had wondered, when he discovered the windmill wasn't a giant after all, but rather an empty-headed little chit who yelled for help, then couldn't make up her infernal mind? Jared had searched about for his sense of humor, but he'd only been able to locate the duke's wig. With what aplomb he could muster, Jared had handed it back to the outraged peer.

Sheffield had blustered in perfect fury, terming Jared a fool, an interfering idiot, a moron. And in complete agreement, Jared for once could not think of a single retort.

Jared pinched the bridge of his nose, closing his eyes at the memory, which stung worse than his injured leg.

"Monsieur is in great pain?" Frontenac asked anxiously. "Shall I fetch some laudanum?"

"No, a large whiskey would be more to the purpose. In fact, the whole bottle." Jared shifted painfully on the mattress. "But instead you'd best go see if you can procure me a pair of breeches."

"I have a clean shirt, a fresh stock, and breeches for monsieur right here, but—"

Jared eyed his valet incredulously. "You brought along a change of clothes for me when we were going to be waylaying coaches?"

"I am always prepared, monsieur. It would be a poor reflection on me if I ever allowed my gentleman to be seen abroad without a decent cravat."

Jared rolled his eyes. "Well, never mind the cravat, but fetch me the breeches at once."

Frontenac's jaw dropped open in horror as Jared swung his legs over the side of the bed. "Monsieur, what are you doing?"

"Getting myself dressed for the ride back to London."

"Monsieur must not think of such a thing!"

"I'm not. I'm doing it." Jared grunted as he eased himself into a standing position. His leg throbbed, but he was relieved to find he could put his weight on it.

Frontenac remonstrated and cajoled, but when he saw it was all to no avail, he turned and fled the room. Doubtlessly afraid Jared would break the wound open and commence to bleeding again, Jared thought dourly.

Though he felt a trifle light-headed, Jared managed to locate his breeches. The worst part was easing the tight fabric up over his bandage, but he managed. He was panting a little from his exertions by the time he began doing up the buttons on the flap.

The door to the room was flung open, and Jared

saw that Frontonac had sent up reinforcements. Maria barged in without ceremony. Hands on hips, she demanded, "Jared Branden, what do you think you are doing?"

"Putting on my breeches. And it is not a performance for which I usually require an audience."

Compressing her lips, she slammed the door behind her. "Get back into bed at once."

One of the servants belowstairs must have lent Maria a gown. The plain brown frock was many sizes too small for her, revealing her shapely ankles, the fabric straining across her bosom tight enough to burst the stitchings. At any other time, Jared would have been more appreciative of the sight.

But doing his best to ignore Maria, he limped around in search of his boots.

Maria strode forward and planted herself in front of him, tossing her disheveled golden hair back over her shoulders. "Jared, did you hear me? You cannot possibly think of going anywhere tonight. Your leg—"

"The merest scratch. Just go ask the good Dr. Marsden. I could not persuade the damn fellow to amputate."

"Amputate!" she gasped.

"Yes, if I'm going to keep getting injured in the same leg, I figured I'd do better to have a wooden one."

"Oh, Jared. I—I am so sorry." Maria bit ruefully down on her lip. "You look so pale. Please come back to bed."

Jared never thought he'd refuse such an invitation from any female, especially not Maria. But he found his boots and sank stiffly down on a wooden chair.

"We have to get back to town," he said. "We can't stay here."

"If you are worried about scandal, it will be all right. I told the landlady we are married. I said we just eloped to escape the machinations of my evil uncle, who is plotting to murder me for my inheritance. But he sent this assassin after us, a Turk, and . . ."

Maria's voice trailed off at Jared's dark look.

"I am not in the mood for any more of your faerie stories, Maria."

Maria winced. She could plainly see that. A grim silence had settled over Jared ever since the fiasco on the Staines Road, a dour mood that Maria did not believe was entirely owing to his wound.

"There is a better reason than scandal for us to be gone," Jared said. "I warned you how vindictive Sheffield can be. He is likely laying a complaint against us. Even now some constable may be searching Hounslow to arrest us."

"I don't think His Grace will do that. Sir Arthur won't let him. He turned out to be a most understanding young man. I feel so guilty for having disliked him before I'd even met him."

Jared made no reply. His lips set in a taut, stubborn line, he attempted to force his foot into his boot.

Kneeling down before him, Maria took the Hessian from his grasp. But instead of helping him with it, she whisked the boot away, saying, "Jared, please. I know you have every right to be angry."

"Who's angry? Just because Miss Lucas has the

bad taste to ruin a perfectly good rescue by falling in love?"

Maria sighed. "I could have shaken the foolish child myself. Not for falling in love, but neglecting to tell us the situation had changed. She could have contrived some way to get word to us. But I suppose all turned out well in the end."

Jared leaned forward and wrenched the boot back from her. "If you can call being made to look a total fool a good end."

"You didn't look foolish, Jared. You were utterly magnificent. You—"

"Just stop it, Maria," he snapped. "I'm not your Count Roberto. You fantasized yourself this imaginary hero, and then you tried to do the same thing with me. Well, it didn't work." He gave over his efforts with the boot and slammed it down instead. Grimacing, he struggled to his feet and stalked a few halting steps away from her.

"The whole thing was a farce from beginning to end. I looked perfectly ridiculous out there tonight."

"It wasn't your fault," Maria cried, scrambling to her feet.

"Yes, it was. I should have known better than to—" He shrugged, his back to her. "I'm not your knight in shining armor, Maria. I will never be the kind of man you want me to be."

Maria crept up behind him, gently touched the rigid set of his shoulder. "You already are."

He wheeled about, his eyes blazing. "Then why the devil is it you only ever want to pretend being married to me? I don't understand. I will never—" He broke off, raking his hand back through his hair. "Why, Maria? Why didn't you come to the church that day?"

There was a quiet anguish in his voice that Maria had never heard before, a despairing expression in his eyes Jared had never revealed. Until that moment, she had never been sure of how much she'd hurt him that long-ago Valentine's Day.

"I—I wanted to come to you that day," she faltered. "But I was afraid."

"Afraid of what?"

"Afraid you didn't really care."

He flung up his hands in an exasperated gesture. "How could you think that?"

"You never spoke of your feelings. When you talked of your reasons for wanting to marry me, you always made jests. I was terrified of making a mistake as dreadful as the one —" Her voice broke, and it was a moment before she finished in a whisper, "As the one my mother made when she married my father."

Jared stared at her, frowning. "But you always led me to believe that—that—"

"That my parents' marriage was perfect. That the reason my father always seemed so cold and distant was because my mother's death broke his heart." Maria shook her head, her eyes blurring with tears. "The truth is that sometimes I fear his unkindness drove her to her grave. Their love match, their devotion to each other. It was just another of my faerie tales, another pretty lie. To deceive the world, and most of all, me."

She swallowed hard before she could continue. "Theirs was a runaway match, consummated in a fit of passion. My father's family strongly disapproved, and he was disinherited. He always thought my grandfather would come round, but he never did. It made my father very bitter, but my mother didn't mind. She continued to adore him, although, over time, he came to despise her. He was so very much more intelligent than she was, you see. Just as you've always been more clever than me—"

"Maria!"

But she resisted the tender note of reproof in his voice, the gentle way he reached out to caress her cheek. The urge to cast herself into Jared's arms was great, but it had taken her so long to be able to admit any of this, she could not stop now.

"Matters only grew worse after I was born," she said hoarsely, "when my father came to realize that the only child he'd ever have was nothing but a useless girl. He never forgave either me or my mother for his disappointment. He could be so cruel." Maria's lips trembled. "Not in a violent way, but with such an acid tongue, the freezing silences."

"Maria, why did you never explain any of this to me before?"

"I was too ashamed, too frightened of your reaction. How could I expect you to love me if my own father never did?"

"You foolish girl." Jared tipped up her chin, looking at her with such tenderness, the tears that shimmered on her lashes escaped to spill over. "Your father was obviously a bitter, twisted old man who could never see what a treasure he possessed. What a beautiful and, yes, very intelligent daughter he had. Instead of being grateful, he chose to live out his life in isolation, wretched and alone. But, Maria, don't force his choice upon me."

"But I was so confused back in those days." Maria dashed her tears away with the back of her hand. "You did not seem distressed when I jilted you." She sniffed. "You were too busy giving Miss King her driving lessons."

"At a place where I knew you'd been bound to see me and hopefully become jealous." He sighed ruefully, gathering her hands into his own. "You were always good at fantasies, Titania. I was good at disguising my feelings. I was just as afraid as you, but of showing any tenderness. I was bred in a family of warriors, you know, not lovers."

"I was excessively grateful for your warlike training tonight. You saved my life. When the duke thought I was a highwayman, I believe he would have run me through, if you hadn't cast yourself in between."

He shrugged. "I don't know much about this hero nonsense, but I do gather it's considered damn careless to allow one's lady to be cut in twain."

"Jared!" Her soft exclamation was part reproof, part plea.

He squirmed a little, then admitted, "All right. I would have rather been pierced through a hundred times before I'd allow Sheffield to touch one hair of your head."

"Why?"

"You know why, you little fool," he said huskily.

"Could you not say it just this once?"

He glanced about as though fearful of being overheard. Looking mighty uncomfortable, he muttered, "I love you."

"What?"

"I said I love you, damn it!"

A glad cry bubbled in Maria's throat. Before she could assure him the feeling was mutual, Jared had taken matters into his own hands. Dragging Maria into his arms, he captured her lips in a ruthless kiss.

It was several breathless moments later before Maria was permitted to speak again. She gazed up at Jared, stroking back one lock of stubborn hair that tumbled over his brow. "There! Now, that really was not so painful, was it?"

"No, it wasn't," he murmured, looking a little astonished. "I love you," he repeated again as though testing the sound of the words. "In fact, given time, I think I could grow to be quite a bore on the subject."

But Maria did not find it in the least boring, especially not when Jared crushed her hard against him, kissing her again until her blood seemed to thunder in her ears.

She melted against him with a sigh of mingled bliss and regret. "Oh, Jared. I have been such a fool. Making us waste ten years of our lives."

"No, Titania. As painful as it was, I fear you were right not to wed me then. It could have been a disaster. You were lost too much in your dream-world, and I didn't dare to dream enough. We were young and foolish."

"And now?" she murmured.

"Oh, now we're middle-aged and foolish. So that should make everything quite all right."

Maria chuckled and sought his lips again. But to her chagrin, he held her at bay.

"No more of that," he said sternly. "Until we get something settled. I can't manage to get down on one knee, but I still want you to marry me, Maria. And this time I'm *asking*."

"Oh, yes," she breathed. "Just name the day and church. I'll be there."

"I know you will, because this time I'll fetch you myself." Before he would kiss her again, he insisted, "And you must promise me one other thing."

"What's that?"

"The next time you drag me out on one of these harebrained rescues, for mercy's sake, Maria, make sure it's really necessary."

"The next time?" she repeated wonderingly. "Will there be one?"

"Knowing you, my dearest Titania, I've no doubt of it." But the wry purse of his lips was belied by the love shining from his eyes.

There was little to be done but seize him by the collar of his shirt and demand that he kiss her again. Jared proved more obliging this time, so much so that tenderness fast blazed into passion.

A delicious shiver worked through Maria and she skated her fingers suggestively over the buttons that fastened his shirt. "Maybe we never will have to fess up to your aunt Clarissa. We could begin working on those seven children very soon."

"In fact, we could start immediately."

It was not until Jared had tumbled her back onto the bed that Maria snapped out of the glow of happiness and desire that enveloped her. She saw him wince as he eased himself down beside her, and she remembered.

Overcome with remorse, she sat up. "Oh, Jared. I have been so selfish, not thinking. Your leg . . . You couldn't possibly . . ."

"Couldn't I?" he retorted, drawing her back into his arms, a wicked smile curving his lips. "Come here, my love, and let me show you just how heroic I can be."